D1243372

ADVANCE PRAISE FOR *LUNGFISH*

"Meghan Gilliss's *Lungfish* is a force of nature—a deeply felt marvel of a book that navigates grief, parenthood, and the mysteries of family with unrelenting power and precision. Here is a story about the islands we build and carry with us. Here is storytelling at its best." —Paul Yoon, author of *Snow Hunters* and *Run Me to Earth*

"*Lungfish* offers up journeys physical and psychic, so it's fitting that it takes place on an island, which is a transitional place. It's about families, past and present, and the lifelines they provide, along with their often tangled confusions. The revelations about the natural world are wonderful, and give a sense of what endures." —Ann Beattie

"Tender, brutal, and faultless on the line, *Lungfish* masterfully explores how estranged family can be as present and punishing as weather. A poetic debut as rich and intentional as the sea." —Marie-Helene Bertino, author of *Parakeet*

"This is a novel about the *real* Maine, one where family and landscape converge to make or break you, where emotions are tied to the weather, to the body, to the past. Meghan Gilliss's exquisite prose and exploratory narrative reflect her main character's searching and conflicted inner dialogue and give rise to a new kind of heroine: an ordinary woman who survives despite everything against her. *Lungfish* is broody and breathtaking, like the Maine coast itself. What a soaring debut!."

—Kerri Arsenault, author of
Mill Town: Reckoning with What Remains

"*Lungfish* is as suspenseful as a thriller, as finely wrought as a poem, and as heartbreaking as a love song. Meghan Gilliss is an extraordinary writer. I loved this book."

—Kate Christensen, author of *The Last Cruise*

"*Lungfish* is a lyrical force, a narrative which moves in rhythm reminiscent of the tide, with sentences that sting in their salty complexity and yet are also soothing, like a balm."

—Makenna Goodman, author of *The Shame*

"At the center of this miraculous and absorbing book is a bracing portrait of a young woman at a pivotal moment in her life. Meghan Gilliss has a rare and electrifying talent for illuminating the precise rhythms of thought and feeling—while also keeping us lovingly immersed in the grit and brine and lucid fascinations of island living. This novel is an absolute treasure."

—Lewis Robinson, author of *Water Dogs*

"In *Lungfish*, Meghan Gilliss has written a remarkable book about motherhood, survival, marriage, lies, money, and drug use. Gilliss' prose is a brilliant light in the darkness the novel explores. This book will haunt me, in the very best way."

—Annie Hartnett, author of *Unlikely Animals*

LUNGFISH

LUNGFISH

A Novel

MEGHAN GILLISS

Catapult
New York

Copyright © 2022 by Meghan Gilliss

First Catapult edition: 2022

ISBN: 978-1-64622-091-5

Library of Congress Control Number: 2021950810

Jacket design by Nicole Caputo
Book design by Wah-Ming Chang

Catapult
New York, NY
books.catapult.co

Printed in the United States of America

1 3 5 7 9 10 8 6 4 2

For Adam and for Ida, without whom
there would be none of it

Little lamb who made thee
  Dost thou know who made thee

—WM. BLAKE, "The Lamb"

SO

AGNES

Agnes—the first Agnes, who was my father's mother, not long dead, on whose island I find myself now, and whom I named my daughter after (if only to pretend to understand a mystery)—had always protected her love for her only child. Sometimes, I sensed, against her husband's counsel.

There was a lack of practical concern that ran in our blood. She might have been the first, my grandmother, or it may have entered sooner—I know so little of those who came before. I never much thought to ask. I never much noticed what wasn't said. Which is to say: By nature, I made do with what was given. By nature, I didn't much notice what wasn't.

Agnes—this Agnes—comes from different stock.

HERE

My body is still and flat beneath the heavy quilts—the smell of them part mothball, part cedar, part mildew, part beach rose, part my grandmother. I'm still not used to sleeping in this bed where she died, beneath her stained glass window—the blues and yellows and reds that form a cross, encircled in the Celtic way. In this bed on this island where no one else lives. In this house halfway out to sea. In this Gulf of Maine. On this island shaped like a shepherd's crook, where pine needles stuck to my feet with sap when I was a child, on the short visits that made each summer a thing that belonged to me.

I try again to imagine having religion. I try again to imagine having religion, and having it watch over my bed—where, presumably, things happen. I imagine having religion and a husband I'm in the habit of touching. I imagine another way of living. But it's a lot to sustain, and it's early, and there's no hope of coffee.

Paul hasn't slept, I'm sure. He paces, or sits with his elbows on his knees and his fists clasped in his hair, and rocks, and trembles. His sweat—a sick slickness that covers the surface of him—carries the smell. Brings it out of his body, like the damp sea air brought it out of the walls.

I do panic a little, knowing he's just outside the door.

I could make myself get up if there was a guarantee that everything else would stay the same. But the sun comes up shockingly fast, like always, and starts it all. The light through the stained glass colors the bedspread. The blues and yellows and reds—watery in their playful shiftiness, in the way they encroach and lap and cover as the branches of the firs out there sway in the breeze—start by my toes and move upward toward my navel. This is when Agnes wakes up and begins to cry for me—at my navel, without fail.

Maaaa-Maa.

My feet hit the stairs. I hear Paul's own steps moving down the hallway, into the room I've just ceded. The bedroom. In turn, he has ceded this: the rest of the house, dancing with its own light. In nearly every window hangs some little glass ornament, refracting. I pause, and listen to the door latch quietly behind him, the *pound pound pound shhh, pound pound pound shhh* as he goes from one end of the room to the other, turning on the ball of his foot. A change of scenery, a room not yet filled with stale air pulled through his body, his hell.

Ma! Ma!

I was late to so much knowledge.

When the giant oak split into four equal parts and fell, and the calm Boniface was not crushed, and the pagans who had previously sung to the earth saw at last what this traveler had claimed all along protected him—this *Father*—how quickly were they absolved of their sin of blindness? Did it matter much how willful it was? If their blindness could have been termed active denial? What if, instead of a loving force, it was a malevolent one being ignored? If Boniface instead allowed himself to be crushed by a tree that was bent on destroying him, to warn the others? As a means of saying: *Look!* Does the concept of innocence become moot in the rush to escape, to survive? Is it moot without a judge? Is it moot, *period*?

There are several categories of books on my grandmother's shelves: Religious texts; field guides; and collections of poetry— barely distinguishable, with their stolid cloth spines and shortened, embossed titles, from the liturgical tomes.

Mysteries line the bottom rows.

Beyond the shelter of our curved little harbor—the grabbing end of the crook—the water is rough; I turn and turn and turn the dory against the chop. I didn't know it was like this today.

Agnes crawls to the starboard side and pulls herself up by the gunwale.

Agnes! I shout. Down!

She drops to the slatted boards and screams. Not because I scared her, I think. Because she's not getting what she wants. It's good she's down low. If she tumbled out, could I go in after her without losing the boat? I'm not a pro. I don't know if you're supposed to have some sort of a license. I keep us on course.

We get to the shore. We get to the car. We get to the city and the library and the internet and the U-Haul where propane is sold—all this civilization.

What's new, now, is everything I didn't see. My life behind the curtain.

HOOK

At dusk, we choose another field guide and walk the paths—hardly discernible from the rest of the woods in this early June—to identify what else is new: the trembling bluets and the poking green leaves of adder's-tongue. And, where we turn toward the beach with our bucket: wood anemone—windflowers, by another name—once thought to open only at the touch of the wind. According to this book. We continue to the beach, to look for supper. Agnes pulls my hand, trying to lead me to the lower reaches, just smoothed by the outgoing tide, where the coppery weed hangs wet over rocks. She knows by now that nothing at the top is fresh enough to eat. But there's a shrub clinging to the edge of the escarpment, with small waxy leaves, and I'm flipping through the book, trying to name it. Her impatience is frequent, and justified. She's pulling my shirt, stretching it. Her hunger, now, makes naming impossible. Her hunger drags me away.

The bulbous capsules at the fringe of the seaweed pop between her teeth as her mouth accepts the slimy brine. She chews up the weed, chewing and chewing. She's not satisfied unless I do it with her. I gag, and try my best to swallow.

I wonder how they helped her, privately. My grandmother. These old stories of men felling trees, et cetera. God knows what else those books contain.

•

At night, Agnes insists on *Rumpelstiltskin*. The book is ancient, the translations direct, unbuffered. Aside from What are Brothers Grimm, she asks no questions. She might as well be a snake digesting a rat. I can see the story moving through. I just can't see what she's doing with it.

In the morning, we shake the skinny trees so the wetness comes down on our heads, our shoulders.

Will Paul be better in four days? Six? Ten?

Here, on a computer in the library in the city, I look at rental prices. For twenty minutes. I think, if I just look at the *next* apartment, maybe it will be the one that's possible. The one that makes things possible. Because what I have learned—what I could have known sooner, if I was looking harder—is that we have no money. None. And only so much time to get off the island before someone finds us out.

Mama! Agnes yells, again.

I know, I say.

What I'm supposed to be looking for, actually—what brought me here—are jobs I can do with a child at my hip. Maybe, seated here, reality hit. The impossibility of it. And this is the way I pivoted: to this other impossible thing, that for some reason felt more possible, for a moment. You get sixty minutes here.

Mama!

I scroll faster, hovering over the keyboard as I stand, apartment listings still flying, unsorted by price now because I'm looking for the one that has slipped through the cracks, the one that only I will find because I'm the one looking at every single listing, even the ones with typos in the price lines, or owners who don't know how to use the platform.

Mama! Agnes yells again, pulling now at the neckline of my shirt.

We'll need some place to go when we're found, or when ice grabs at the rocks, at the pipes running through the house, at the dory—tries to pry apart its wooden boards, seize its puny propeller; when the thin walls, made for summer, are nothing against the shrieking cold, and a single misstep could mean death. The inability to get a fire going, hands too cold to strike a match. Or simple failure to rouse. They say the process of freezing to death is like being lulled into a dream. A capsize amid the winter swells in a necessary trip to shore: for food, for water, for gas to cook with.

It's June now. The storms that break mooring chains begin in October. But Law can stake its claim whenever.

She left this place to my father. My grandmother.

My father is nowhere to be found.

Seen last in Indiana, en route to Mexico, before I finished high school.

Perhaps she thought this place would bring him back. Perhaps that was her gift.

•

You wonder if the birds feel it, too, at dawn—the notion that any direction is just as well—when the water is as pink as the sky. I'll bring Agnes next time, so she can see it too. What she has seen, already, is how at night, the house—with the kitchen light burning—is like a glow at the back of a very dark throat.

Take shower? she says, when I've hurried back. And off we go, shaking trees.

I've not yet told the executor how long my father's been gone. I don't yet know if this process—wherein his absence is realized—is one I should want to speed up, or slow down. My instincts say, Reveal nothing. Use this time.

My grandmother once told me that, not so unexpectedly, lobsters' hearts slow down as the ambient temperature falls—slowing more, the colder it gets. But that small devices implanted in a study group revealed occasional spontaneous beats—completely unpredictable—from the heart of each lobster. As if two systems are at odds with each other, one attempting to override the other, my grandmother said. What do you think that other system is? she asked me.

The magazines, as they've always been, are in a stack beside the woodstove. Burned in no particular order that I can glean. Going back to 1988. In each of them, her name is listed with the handful of others thanked for their foundational support.

She had no reason to think I wasn't able to pay my bills. That I was *in need*. Even if I'd known in time, it's unlikely I would have told her. She'd already given me a gift, the money for school, the first time, and I'd wasted it.

Drop it! I yell, in the brilliant sun.

Agnes is coming toward me on the beach, her finger wedged into the little cross-slit at the tip of the plastic tampon applicator she's found washed up. She's screaming because she thinks it's biting her, and she's angry.

There is nothing that scares her.

In my in-box is another query from the executor, wondering again if I can't provide any additional information that could help him locate my father. There's a thumbnail photo alongside his email signature, and I see again that it's the worst case, though it's not completely without pity that I see it: his tamed-down hair, the suit a little much, a forced ease, a guy on the hook by generations. A guy whose task is to see this property vest, who must order a world through contracts with the dead.

Again, I don't reply.

Again, I write to my father.

Is Yahoo even a thing, anymore?

I imagine the day he finally sits at a computer. I imagine what he'll learn, if he hasn't already. He has a granddaughter. His mother is dead. His son is, of all places, overseas. There's a vast trap of bureaucracy waiting to drop down on him. I'm afraid it will be too much. The notes I leave are like seeds, leading to the palm of my hand. I hope I can keep him calm enough to catch him. There are tiny offerings I can trace back to Agnes's birth.

Her eyes are gray.

You should hear her voice—she sounds like a dove that smokes. A smoking dove.

I get the feeling, sometimes, that she knows more than me.

Not written: *When we found the wood anemones, she bent down to face one and said, Any money? Because it didn't answer, she plucked off its head and chewed it, before she spat it out.*

It's not really seeds I'm offering. It's Agnes.

How can she not be enough for these men?

Apple, I tell her. I'm going to eat you now. I'm sorry. I begin on her soft belly, holding her up as we leave the library by way of the sliding glass doors.

Driving out of town, back up the coastal road, my eyes fall on the gas needle. I stare back at the road.

Some part of me, it seems, still thinks that this will do it. Ignoring critical indicators. Imagining that anything is fine.

The propane tank, nearly four feet tall, is buckled into the passenger seat. Agnes is buckled into the seat behind it, in her car seat. Not ideal, I realize. But necessary. Until Paul comes out of his rooms, having shaken and sweated and shitted it all out, it's up to me. Until he's back in his skin, restored.

FORCED

I can't say for sure she planned it—if she felt it coming and made the necessary arrangements. I only know that the boy who ran her fuel and groceries once a week found her in her bedroom. This bedroom. I only know her body was beneath the heavy quilt with the big red star at its center, dressed in a thin blue nightgown and one of my dad's old flannel shirts, left years ago, because that is how I imagine it.

What I know, for sure, is this: She got her float in early, making the mooring guy get out in the cold chop and wind. He pulled back the tarp that covered the yellow dory to scrape its belly clean of last year's barnacles, a mix of salt water and blood running through the grooves of his knuckles. He rolled the heavy wooden boat off its piles beneath the shelter of pines and swept the spiders out. He hauled the six-horsepower motor down from the shed and dropped it into the well behind the bench, pushing the whole heavy thing back into the water, towing it over to the mainland where it could wait for her to arrive.

I'd always loved the way her face opened to the wind. As my child's does. I try to relax my muscles, to not be so ugly and clenched. I grip the throttle.

Her last letter to me, written from here, said that for the first time in her life she was going to sit and watch the fiddleheads push through the thick blanket of needles, despite all advice. *I can't pretend to know this place any longer, when I only see it fully dressed.* She was disoriented without the foliage, she admitted; it was a place she'd thought she could navigate blind. Its paths, its fallen trees, its little humps of granite bulging from the soil just before the curve above the marsh—this is what she saw, when she closed her eyes, when she returned to the Delaware house she'd shared with her husband. But twice now already she'd been someplace other than where she thought she was, and had a quick feeling of being lost, a kind of vertigo, as she tried to locate herself. The distances felt off— too much ground in some places, not enough in others, she said. She was eighty-four, but being here, now, I'm certain age had nothing to do with it. It's a confusing place, early—even now, when some of the foliage has begun to hide the earth, the sky, the bits we're unaccustomed to seeing.

I hadn't visited since my father left, though it's true, too, that she never offered an invitation. Distances felt off, without him there between us. But she always wrote.

In Pittsburgh, that strange, failed home, a pale sun had done weak battle with the mounds of dirty snow and ice for several weeks. On the Friday when I got the news, it came out hot and strong; Agnes and I sat in the grass of a sorry playground and picked at tiny purple flowers, the groundwater soaking our bottoms.

Per Agnes's instructions, someone none of us knew interred her remains quietly beside her husband's, inside the wall of a church.

On her nightstand here, where I'll leave it, is *The Black Prince*, by Iris Murdoch. A paperback from the seventies, yellow pages.

We can make ourselves crazy, trying to know someone.

CATCH

The way my father's location is unknown feels different from the way my mother's is. He isn't *gone*. At least, he wasn't. Not until now, when I need him.

Conrad, my brother, was a freshman at our high school when Dad became bent on working as a laborer at a resort in Mexico. After that, it was just the two of us living at the house in Birdseye, where we grew up—a center point between Patoka Lake, Temple, Sassafrass, and Jasper, going clockwise around the gut of Indiana. Not too far from I-64 to Corydon, then Louisville across the river. Mom had already left us. Dad thought this idea, like others, was perfect—a work of art. He thought someone—I'm not sure who exactly—was watching. All our lives, he'd taken us to Louisville whenever there were court steps to stand on, banners to wave. Once, when the KKK held a rally, and we as protesters were channeled into a fenced-in protest zone, and patted down for weapons, he became so argumentative with the police about the principle of it, those monsters out there marching free, that he ended up in jail for the night. Since Conrad was only seven and I was only ten, Mom had to come and get us.

Dad wrote from Mexico to say he was staying a little longer. Then a little longer still. The letters kept coming and he stopped mentioning a return.

He stopped telling us exactly where he was—not a

conscious omission, I didn't think, just like such a thing had lost significance. He might have stopped keeping track of it himself. He wrote instead about people he'd met, and the flora—the brainlike fruit of the pitaya, the useful maguey, the ahuehuete as wide as a house—and the way you could live out of doors and not bother about clothes or all the things we thought we needed. How you could let the world take care of you. He seemed to be heading farther and farther south; mountains rose up in his ramblings; I could tell he was cold by the way his sentences tightened. He wrote of the smell of boiling wool; of colors that stained his hands. Unfamiliar things.

Whatever disillusionment he suffered at the resort, it didn't send him home. There was never anything wrong with his ideas, when they failed. Only things wrong with the world. He went deeper, looking for an even different world. Of course I wasn't mad.

Conrad and I took turns cooking the meals. I did most of the laundry. There were no horses to take care of anymore, and the raspberries around the periphery encroached on the unmown field that teemed with bugs—grasshoppers and funnel-web spiders and ticks. When Conrad had a fever that wouldn't break and I could barely wake him up, I took him to an Urgent Care down the highway and they put him on doxycycline and he couldn't go in the sun for two weeks. We got jobs to pay the rent, to keep the lights on.

Then I went to college. Or, to be more precise, to horse school—the tuition a gift from my grandmother, who rarely thought money was a reasonable solution to anything, was any better than learning to live; she had made loans to my father, I knew, but only when the circumstances were dire. Until Mom left, these were the only times I heard him cry, and beg.

Conrad was on his own. He didn't have trouble with the bills because he dropped out of high school and picked up cash work.

The letters from my father arrived at the house less frequently. The ones that did come looked like they'd been through floods, my brother said, when I called from my dorm. Cockfights. They contained no real news, but seemed important in their own way; lacked clarity, but were packed with a kind of urgency. I settled on thinking he just needed to show he hadn't abandoned us. And needed to know we knew he was alive.

So there is *some* need that is not totally tended by the world down there, I remember thinking.

REMEMBER

I rocked it up the gangplank, and now I'm rocking it up the hill, inch by inch, back and forth, sweating. It's too big. It's only half full. I can't lift it. How can propane be so heavy?

Mama!

What? I say, too sharply. She's been good. She stood right where I told her to on the bucking dock while I wrestled the tank into the dory so I only had to imagine what it would be like if she slipped between the boat and dock as the waves pushed everything together, a hundred-pound tank thrown into the mix to shake things up.

I love you like thunder.

Like thunder?

I let the lip of the tank sink an inch into the loose soil, the bed of fallen pine needles that make a path up to the house.

The fact of Agnes, sometimes, leaves me floored. I drop to my knees and pull her in. I feel her heartbeat, fast and steady, against my chest.

To mark her birthday, I turn her into a cake. Out on the beach, in the full sun, I cover her with sand and stick two razor clams into the mound. She's been two for three months already; I just feel like celebrating, again.

ERROR

It was Paul's idea to come here. He knew I would. And not just to get away from whatever was wrong in Pittsburgh—the gaps in his presence I couldn't make sense of, more and more of them since the birth of Agnes, into whom I was able to disappear, in return, with shocking ease. My hunger.

I considered another woman. A co-worker, if I had to guess. I hoped it would stop. I didn't know how to ask him without sounding horrible, without hating myself, without making everything worse. I couldn't imagine anything I wanted to be less than a new mother with a husband who'd moved on.

And part of me really didn't believe he could do it. Part of me believed the things he said. They were the things he had always said, that had made me love him—there were just so many more of them now. He missed dinner because he'd rescued a bird, a little starling, a trash bird, that flew into his office window—drove it out to a raptor rescue, in the country. He didn't call at lunch because he'd walked with a dementia patient he encountered on the sidewalk, and talked with her about her son, the lawyer, who was just then at his first day of kindergarten, who she worried about because he was so much smaller than the other boys, until someone from her home came and picked her up—he'd suspected something was off because she had asked him to refill her water, and held up one of those tiny paper cups for pills. I can't wait to love you when you're like that, he said to me. He missed bedtime because he'd given a co-worker a ride home, blew two tires passing the place where the new detention center was being built, and sat with the tow truck driver an extra hour in the cab while the man asked Paul if he'd done the right thing, keeping his child who had spinal muscular atrophy. He had seven children already, and life was tough. This last child, as much as he loved her—maybe even more than the others—just might be the thing that destroyed them.

But really, Paul had never slept with someone he didn't love.

He knew I would come here because it's my favorite place, and I might never be able to come again.

My grandmother's ashes had been in the wall for a week when he brought it up.

What about your job? I said. Our lease?

You're unhappy. I miss you.

To which there might have been a wiser response than joy. And hope. And agreeing it made sense to sell our belongings and take only what would fit in the car.

HUSH

My dinghy glides onto the bed of purple dulse that's lying flat on the surface of the water at this half tide—the drag of the tendrils brings us to a stop as I pull in the oars. There was a period when the world was trying to tell me something. When I was ignoring what it had to say. When Agnes cried at my nipple. When the mailbox, too, stayed empty. I know, I say now. I know, I know, I know. It's old news, but thank you.

It's just sunny enough to see the variation in the colors. Violet, indigo. Bright, shiny russet. Agnes watches as I unsheathe the machete. The blade is long and hard to maneuver underwater, but I've had some practice now. I pull the sliced-off tendrils—slippery, chaotic garlands—into the boat.

On the floor, the seaweed titters—it sounds like gossip, from the world down there, and I have to grin. By the time I've gotten us back to the dock, the tittering has nearly ceased—I know it's just a matter of what water there was having seeped out by now through tiny fissures—but still, it's hard to not make more of the quiet, to take it as the hush of doom. Agnes works on another mouthful. I'll try boiling it tonight; it's pretty tough as is.

Hang on, Apple, I say—though I've tried to expunge the nickname, which was never meant to stick.

•

I try to prod the creature—a dark, strange-moving shape—away from the road, away from me, but the stick won't move right. It moves like the machete underwater. The animal doesn't belong here, and I don't know why it keeps coming toward me. I give up, and try instead to yell, and wake up.

The sky, too, is awake. Rumbling. Low, constant, then sudden.

Like thunder, I think.

Love, like grief.

What made her put such faith in her own seed-in-palm? This island as offering?

FIRST

LEISURE

Her cheek was pressed against the warm wood of the porch. Next to us was the crisp-edged feather I'd run up and down her spine until I was sure she was dreaming. A year earlier, there'd been no freckles on her back. Now there were three, clustered by her shoulder blade. There was also one on the bridge of her nose, and one on the soft skin just beneath her eye. We'd been on the island two days.

What I was still not used to was so much afternoon sun on the porch, such openness right in front of the house. I'd been here the summer the big trees—the tall, straight cedars—were brought down, but not since.

Earlier, in bed, Paul had leaned over to kiss my forehead, perfunctory, before I'd woken up, and it was his shadow I registered first, as it moved over me, then his voice, telling me he was going ashore.

In the car, driving here, state after state, we'd talked about what we wanted. What time we could get on the island, a new job for him, then a little place in the country, the way I liked. Life in balance again. His eyes scanned the edge of the highway for exits.

You all right?

Have to pee.

The fields stretched on. An Amish boy walked a horse toward a barn. The silence widened. Paul had forgotten me. I

climbed into the back seat to entertain Agnes, scooting aside
the duffel bag containing all that was hers in the world.

Agnes was in dreamland. The feather was banded—an os-
prey's, brown and white. I watched the two nest mates above
the trees, down toward the eastern shoreline. They were riding
the currents, slow arcs out over the water and back; they didn't
seem to be looking for much, not really, just practicing their
flight. I picked up the feather and brought it down, turned the
rachis a dial and brought it down again—this time I could feel
the resistance.

It was noon and there was time in that sun.

Two days earlier, when we arrived, there were cool ashes in
the woodstove. Her canvas sneakers—two small, rough holes
carved out by the jut of her biggest toes, by her thick, untended
toenails—perched on a chair beside it. A porcelain cup with
a dried amber ring at its bottom sitting in the enamel basin
of the sink; I picked it up and smelled the brandy. A kettle
half full of cold water on the stove. A single familiar hand
towel—yellow, a pattern of blue irises—out on the line, a few
others in the grass where they'd blown. Gas in the generator
tank. Some dry beans and a few cans of brown molasses bread
in the pantry, a knifelike loaf of sourdough on the table. A
wedge of cheese in the fridge, hard and yellow along its edges.
A single enormous pickle. A wilted sprig of dill in a cup of
half-evaporated water on the windowsill behind the sink; the
glass cloudy and green where the water had been. Her body

had been moved by water ambulance. It was hard to imagine strangers in her bedroom, anyone here who wasn't one of us. But someone had pulled the quilt back up over the pillows once her body was removed from the bed, someone had run their hand over the cotton batting until it lay flat and smooth.

I'd turned the knob on the stove, smelled the propane, and struck a match. I found a box of black tea, Twinings, in the cabinet. I used the water my grandmother had last brought to boil.

A catch: Upon arrival, the dory had been on its island mooring, a possibility we'd considered, but hoped against. But it made sense—the ambulance had fetched her body. She hadn't rushed herself ashore, to be saved at some hospital. She died on a Monday. Was found on Wednesday. In her pillbox, on the bathroom countertop, were pills from *W*, *Th*, *F*, *Sa*, *Su*, and *M*. Only the little lid of *T* was unfastened, its corresponding box empty. The last ones to make it down her throat. Six days of lids clasped shut.

Paul stripped down and swam from the mainland dock through the frigid water to the dinghy, on its mooring there, the only one, his weight nearly tipping the little boat as he clambered into it. He came back for his clothes. Heart stopped for a minute there, he said, hopping on one foot, then the other, getting back into his pants. This was fun. I pointed again to the island that was ours—the long low profile of it about two miles out, the hump of raised ground at its center. He rowed while Agnes and I walked the beach and dipped our toes in the water, me recoiling, Agnes pulling me farther in, our boxy old Volvo crammed with belongings at the top of the hill behind us, and watched small waves displace shiny bits of shell, the sun catching the opalescent fragments as they tumbled, an inch toward us, then an inch away, and catching on the stern of the white dinghy as it grew smaller and smaller, until I couldn't see it, and I was glad Paul had gone to camps as a boy, had been sent away, and jealous, too, that he got to have this natural strength in his arms. Hopeful that he had enough. Two miles, on live water, wasn't nothing. Finally, the yellow bow of the dory came into view. Could I have done that, the way he did, knowing nothing of the ocean or outboard motors or ridiculous old banana-shaped boats? Certainly not with a child climbing all over me.

It was heart death first, most likely. The rush of her unregulated blood too much. Creating a blockage that deprived that muscle of what it needed.

It hurt—that it was five days until I knew.

My job was to reimagine what our life could be. To show Agnes how to whistle a perwinkle out of its shell. To listen to the throaty utterances of seals at night—so close they might as well be inside our heads—and make a choice: Believe something wonderful, or horrible. To show her life, outside of an apartment.

Paul's job was to go ashore, find work. Make it all possible.

I squeezed the rachis, opalescent like a dog's claw, and about the same girth, and wondered what hole was left in the bird.

FAMILIAR

I smelled my grandmother on the blanket in the mornings, after the night's worth of body heat made a sort of steam collect in the wool; I smelled her on my skin.

I smelled my father, too, when the tide was out and the mud squelched between our toes, offering up what the gulls circled for above—limp crabs and loose mollusks, baking alongside everything else too small to see, bodies already crushed and pulled apart into indiscernible bits.

I smelled my brother in the smooth-barked oak on the high ground above the marsh, where what I'd identified from the field guides as trillium grew that time of year. As kids, we'd always come later, by which time the ferns had grown in and filled the dip, their glut of green fronds choking out what I now saw was the rest: the trillium, the fungus-laddered hunks of fallen trees. I smelled him on my hands.

Agnes didn't like being left on the ground alone.

Relax, Apple, I said. I'm coming.

She screamed until I actually did.

I didn't smell my mother.

•

Agnes, I remind myself. *Agnes, Agnes, Agnes.* We're in the real world, with Paul.

The sun hit a place, the sky took on a certain hue, and there I was again, waiting.

FAMILIAR

Something smelled of foreign dirt, of musk and sour damp, of things I did not understand. In Pittsburgh, I thought it was the apartment, something left behind by the previous tenant, like the greasy stain on the wall above the bed. Like the stack of VHS pornos atop the high kitchen cabinet. Here, against everything familiar, I knew it must have followed us, and could almost name it. The dampness held by the house kept it intact almost long enough, seemed to cup it. Hold it out for me. I waited until he was gone—ashore—then looked in every place again.

I could almost name it, and then—

Gone.

Paul came home, beaten down, eager not to talk.

Familiar.

It takes time, Tuck, he said. What is it you want? Everything at once?

I wanted groceries, mostly. Milk, fruit, oatmeal. I would have enjoyed one of those frozen pizzas loaded up with fake meat—dark little nuggets like rabbit pellets, but delicious. The kind of pizza he brought home and watched me put away when I was pregnant. The kind he brought home until he didn't, when maybe the sight of this hunger began to scare him. The kind I became embarrassed to ask for, once Agnes was no longer inside my body. When my hunger was only mine.

What I found, in an upstairs closet, were the three large sunken boxes that had occupied the floor space of the dark blue Dodge, on our last drive up with Dad. The ones that displaced my feet, for seven states, Indiana to here. A dozen years ago. The year the cedars came down.

There was Agnes, stretching a cobweb over the dried husk of a spider on the floor. Tucking it in. For a nap, did she think? Or did she know?

Before her, I depended on no one.

Before her, I took care of myself.

Agnes took me by the hand to the porch and bade me lie down, and put a pillow from a deck chair under my head, and draped a blanket over my middle.

For what is idolatry, if it be not to worship the gifts instead of the giver himself? John Calvin. From the *Biography of*. From the third row of shelves at the base of the stairs.

Also from Calvin: *We must recollect that God would never have suffered any infants to be destroyed except those which He had already reprobated and condemned to eternal death.* This in response to a troublesome psalm, in defense of the full-scale slaughter of God's defectors. *Happy shall he be that taketh and dasheth thy little ones against the stones,* the verse goes.

I can see the dot on the page where she held her pencil in balance—a dark, heavy mark, a fainter tail when she finally pulled it away, having made no comment.

In real religion, it seems, you have to take the bad with the good.

TYGER

He still wasn't home and our hunger had us agitated, fighting each other. Paul had said he'd stop at the supermarket. The sun was about to hit its place in the sky; I took Agnes into the uniform dimness of the house to avoid it. I looked for something to read to her. The book I pulled was clothbound and dark, like most of them—as I turned it over, the light from the window caught the embossed letters of the spine in a coppery flash: *Wm. Blake.* Its bottom edges pressed into the flesh above my knees. Agnes coiled into my lap, behind it, sick of fighting me.

> *And what shoulder, & what art,*
> *Could twist the sinews of thy heart?*
> *And when thy heart began to beat,*
> *What dread hand? & what dread feet?*
>
> *What the hammer? what the chain,*
> *In what furnace was thy brain?*
> *What the anvil? what dread grasp,*
> *Dare its deadly terrors clasp?*

And that was it. I knew it was.
The musk—the smell I'd been tracking.
Tyger.

Agnes's head was on the pillow she'd dragged to the yard—I'd lain with her, per her orders, faking patience, until she was sleeping. I again pulled the shirts out of his drawer. Shook loose the blankets in the cedar chest. Crouched to look under his side of the bed. Lifted up the mattress. Opened the drawers of my grandmother's writing desk. Flapped open every cupboard. Shined my flashlight into the damp crawl space. As if a tiger could fit into any of these tiny lairs. But it was so close. It was with me. This musk that had followed us here.

I prowled the house.

In pencil, scrawled atop the wooden surface of her desk: *Bread, 8:oo.*

Did *everyone's* life revolve around food? Was I making too much of it?

When Agnes woke up, I tried to let myself be pulled back toward her. To leave behind whatever it was I'd become. I billowed one of his loose shirts down over her head like a net, refolded it on the bed once she broke free, plucked up another from the floor while she carried the first to his drawer and laid it flat with a care that startled me.

WHAT HAND

How fucking hard could it be? To locate a tiger?

I remembered my old cat, before the fox got her, the way she slunk against a wall when exiting a room.

This thing, though, I thought—it must have secret doors. Portals to its native bush. Here long enough to upset reality, then gone.

I smelled the cushions. I smelled the heavy curtain that hung to the side of the kitchen doorway. I smelled the water that came from the faucets. I smelled my shirt.

In better moments, I wondered if I'd invented it out of loneliness.

But I smelled it. I did.

And where the fuck was Paul? The beans were long gone. The brown bread. The cheese. The pickle had always been too questionable to touch. Didn't he know this? Did I have to inform him that people need to eat?

LET THE WORLD TAKE CARE OF YOU

I boiled green crabs the size of nickels.

I boiled devil's tongue.

I roasted devil's tongue in pans on the rocks.

We ate devil's tongue raw.

I boiled bladder wrack to make a broth. I did this with knotted wrack, too, for variety.

I wondered if my daughter would always be so wild. I watched her eat ferociously, but I needed her to grow.

How did I end each day shy of my hunger, uncertain of its validity?

MYSTERY

Agnes had been three months old, and I considered my loneliness a weakness—it felt unfemale. I didn't want to mention it. She was asleep in a sling across my chest—would sleep only this way—and I was slowly washing the afternoon's dishes at the sink in front of the Pittsburgh window, which is to say, washing peanut butter off three different spoons, when I saw movement outside in the dusk, a shifting of shadows among the dead brown leaves along the edge of the boggy overgrowth between buildings, and I strained my eyes against the growing dark, watching the shadows as they merged and spread, until it was too dark out there to differentiate anything, and I knew I'd decipher nothing. I half hoped Agnes would stay asleep, half hoped she'd wake up and look at me with her eyes that were still as gray as my grandmother's Atlantic, like she hadn't come entirely into this world out of the other just yet.

Where could he be, at 7:48 p.m., when I had news of a strange animal, and a child another day old I wanted to share with him?

It was amazing: The aloneness a thing you never noticed until, actually, it was gone. Until you weren't alone anymore. Until there was a child with you.

•

There had been parts of seconds in which the colors had begun to separate, and shadows had begun to split, and it had looked like a rodent on tall legs.

The next time I saw it, I tore down the three flights of the fire escape, the door to the kitchen left open, Agnes still on a blanket on the kitchen floor—this was the most distance there'd been between us, ever. I could hear her cries.

It was there, for a second, before it hopped into the brush.

Bird, or rodent?

Maybe this was the way it was always going to be.

Maybe you ducked out of the world for a moment to become a mother and then the joke was on you. The line between species had vanished. The known world had vanished.

We'd given up our internet, to save, before she was born, though he was making decent money; we could usually pick up a neighbor's open signal, slow as it was. But now that signal was gone. Poof. Who knows. I did not know our neighbors, but I knew what they called their Wi-Fi, the names that appeared next to the little closed padlocks, down the row. *GameOrDie*. *MilitiaMilitia*. *Giddyupgirl27*. *Smokescreensteve*.

It was a long hot walk to our little brick branch of the library. Agnes was strapped in her place against my chest. Between us was a slick of sweat—hers or mine, hers and mine, there really was no way to tell.

In a back corner, I picked a field guide from among the rest. I showed Agnes a picture of a red-tailed hawk, then one of a tufted titmouse, then one of a warbler, and she began to quiet down. I told her we were going to look at every picture of every bird until we found the one. And if that didn't work, we'd get a book of rodents instead. She wrapped her fist in my hair. I sat down at a long table and started on the first page, my head at a tilt to accommodate her grip.

Two military helicopters rumbled low over the island. Even the ospreys, who squawk at everything, were quiet.

Let's check on the snails, I said to Agnes, and carried her under the cover of trees. I carried her because she would not follow; she wanted to stand in the clearing and gape up at these earth-shaking intruders. I turned so her screams weren't right inside my head.

Later, inside, it seemed like time to turn the radio on. To spare a little electricity. I could have used the batteries from my flashlight, drop them in, but I still hadn't found what I was looking for. My musky companion. The interloper. The source. I didn't want to risk losing my light. When I was a kid here, there'd always been a shelf in the pantry stocked with batteries of all sizes. I guessed my grandmother had stopped restocking. I guess sometimes you know the end is near. I shook the dust bunnies loose from the cord and plugged the radio into the wall.

The generator was powered by diesel we'd have to replace, bring over from the mainland in big red jugs.

We were not at war, as far as I could tell—not here, not

urgently. Not with all this news of tax reform and firings, absurd appointments and cruel ineptitude. They would have mentioned a war. These antics couldn't bury a domestic siege.

The helicopters, then—they could have been anything. Not for me to know.

I unplugged the cord.

Could those antics bury a domestic siege? Some nefarious government action, in this far-flung reach? I listened again, in three-minute intervals.

I searched the same pockets, the same drawers, the same closets, while Paul and Agnes slept. I made it easy for him to go straight to bed, when he returned bearing nothing. You look so tired, I said. No need to talk. No need to make something up. No need for me to wrap my brain around something he said, choose what to believe. I needed him asleep.

But I looked at him sleeping. His mouth hung open. Why should he be released from this problem? What dreams was he having that he didn't deserve? What knowledge did he disappear with? Why the fuck didn't he share this hunger?

The constriction in my stomach was sharp, the fog encasing my pancake of a brain thick. Over the top of it, something darted frantically, back and forth, hitting the same wall of my skull at each end.

•

We climbed the high ground at the center of the island and
watched the distant sailboats. It was the cannon fire that lured
us. See that one? I said. The sideways one?

Fast! Agnes said.

It was at its vanishing angle. I raised my eyebrows to show
her it was dangerous as well as exciting.

We kept our eyes on the dark brown sail that was just
barely not touching the water. I didn't want to miss the moment. The boat righted.

What would we do if the executor came? Run? Hide among
the trees? Dip ourselves down into the cold water?

How many different ways were there for us to disappear?

Is starvation evident in bone remains? This would be the
best spot, right here. Enough sun to bleach us clean, before we
were found. By some kayaker's dog. Or real estate agent.

Mama?

Hi, Apple. Such a pretty day.

A woman couldn't smell like that, not really. The musk. The
wet floor of another forest. Couldn't leave it all over. Not so
quickly. It would take more time for her smell to get into
things. My grandmother had been here for decades, had crin-
kled the dried petals of the beach roses into the drawers of her
dresser for a lifetime.

But still. Something.

So tiger.

For then. For want. In the damp museum of smells, this
house.

AUDIENCE

We stretched our bodies on the sun-warmed wood of the dock, and even then it wasn't far, just up in the trees, watching us. This third presence. I fished a clump of floating rockweed out of the water, and split it in two. I draped the two slippery pieces over our heads.

We're so beautiful! I said. Look how fancy we are! They should put us in a painting in a fancy museum!

Agnes thought we needed more. I leaned back into the water, felt the cold lapping the soft interior of my elbow.

My fingers grabbed the slick drifting tendrils that I then draped over my hair, being such a good mother.

I pretended to be asleep before Paul came home. Until after it was dark. Until he still hadn't come, and I lay there for hours, mixed up, now, about who I was trying to fool.

It was the BBC, at that strange hour. Reporting on a storm down the American coast. The reporter, with his British accent, was telling us of the mayor of the small American seaside town, inhabited mainly by retirees who had worked hard all their lives to afford themselves these mobile homes along the vastly changing shoreline, advising the residents who wouldn't evacuate to write their names on their arms with Sharpie.

There couldn't have been more than a gallon of fuel left in the generator—I wasn't checking. Not until he came back.

I turned the radio off.

He thought we were what—fine?

I wondered if we were. I couldn't decide if it was beside the point.

I wondered if the boat was out of gas. If he was stuck ashore or adrift in the ocean.

Our phones, of course, hadn't been active in months. Another thing, like the hunger, that he did not see as a problem. That I tried not to see as a problem, even back in the city, when my reluctance to be totally alone with my child made me feel like a bad mother. When I thought the problem was me.

I could be totally, utterly alone with Agnes, and be fine. Then, as now.

When we woke, I dug down into the wet sand of the low beach, and watched her face as our little hollow filled back up with water, from nowhere.

By the time we heard the motor, what had felt urgently wrong in the middle of the night felt normal. Maybe because the hours contained days. He didn't always come home at night; that was now the way of our world.

•

A woodcock. That's what the creature was. Between our building and the next, in Pittsburgh. We found it in the book. Also called a timberdoodle, a Labrador twister, a night partridge, and a bog sucker. Bog sucker!

Their eyes are set far back on their heads so they can keep a watch over things while they stick their long bills into the earth to probe for food.

Even after the females nest down with their offspring, biological imperative accomplished, the males keep on doing it. Keep spiraling high, high, high into the air, again and again, twittering their wings for good measure, for their female down below. They'd already mated.

With those ridiculous bodies, you had to hand it to them.

You had to wonder what they were trying to distract the mothers from.

Exhausted, he said. He dropped a plastic grocery bag onto the kitchen table. For you.

I nodded once, staring at the wall behind him.

The fleet had scurried to the forefront of my skull, their tiny feet scratching over the useless plate, and now they were scratching at the bone. But the fog was far too thick in there, and soon they were scratching at everything, lost.

He left the room. I peeked into the bag, carefully, so he wouldn't hear the plastic rustle.

Graham crackers. Peanut butter. Instant noodles. Half a gallon of cheap milk. All the kinds of things that could be purchased from a gas station.

He did me the favor of staying in the bedroom while Agnes

and I had our feast. I slurped up a package of noodles, then another, until it was clear the sharpness in my stomach wasn't going away. That it needed something else. I smeared peanut butter onto one cracker, and then another.

Agnes appeared content, chasing down each messy bite with a purposeful chug of milk. Until, abruptly, I made her stop, knowing we'd run out.

In the morning fog: odors lifted and hung.
He was gone again, of course.
I tracked the scent until I lost it.

Tyger Tyger, burning bright,
In the forests of the night;
In what drawers or cracks you hide,
Or in what fissures of my mind?

In the darkness, it wafted above him. I leaned over him in the bed, over his open, drooling mouth. It seemed to exude from his molars. There was an element of rot, it struck me—like organic matter decomposing beneath the more freshly fallen leaves. Did he need, on top of everything, to go to the dentist? In fact, maybe that was all it was. Tooth rot. Maybe he had no idea how to tend to this thing by himself, and was suffering in incredible pain, needing me.

Maybe I'd been so tied up being a mother, I'd forgotten to be a wife.

In the morning, he was gone.

•

And then, though it had just been there, hanging in the air, the
smell was gone.

I was left in the doorway holding his jacket, like a towel I'd
just used to wash my face.

They were everywhere—small butterflies the color of, well,
butter. In the full sun they flitted against the beach roses.

I'd already told her we could make tea, the way my grandmother used to. I'd told her how twisty our faces would get.
How good it would make us feel. But there were no rose hips
yet. Just these lovely flowers, their petals broad and white and
fragrant. And these winged things batting around.

It's not that I outwardly believed that butterflies were spies
from hell, recording all our errors. It's that I knew other people believed this once. Before we learned to know better.

We'd gone at the peanut butter, Skippy, for breakfast. We'd
finished it. We liked the way the sugary globs became slick
on our tongues, the way we could cradle them there. The way
our sweet, thick saliva gave us a feeling of fullness, the way
it coated our clamor. I watched my hand lie still—so different from the shaking hand that had twisted and fumbled and
dropped the bright blue lid.

BEHIND

Undeniable. Tiger. Its watch and heft and silence palpable.

It came on a breeze from down the hall. I stopped at something on the wall. A nautical chart of the bay from 1890. There were hundreds of these islands stretched along the coast— there we were: tiny, hooked. I touched us with the tip of my finger. I lifted the bottom edge of the heavy frame away from the wall.

They spilled out, pink and slippery. Like things just born back there. Too many of them, horrid, sliding against each other, multiplying in midair. But not animal. Plastic. Little plastic sheaths cascading, then lying still on the floor.

HANDS

Each bag had a rectangular label, imparting nothing of any bearing. The only meaningful words, *not for human consumption*. The best thing to do was smell their residue—all that was left—and confirm the familiarity, *the closeness, the thing that's been prowling*, then count them twice, with shaking hands.

Eighty-two.

After sixteen days on the island.

Best thing to do: Lay them out, sixteen in a row, then move back to the beginning, laying out another sixteen. And so on. Like laying out a game of memory. A math problem: How many packets per day?

About five.

A math problem that delays, for a moment, the other things.

The single sharp bark of laughter, the slow, painful drawing of air through lungs that are now bricks instead of balloons.

Looking up at the place you love, and seeing it as something else, something it's been since you got here, unperceived.

Knowledge of how little is known. Of how dumbly you've acted. Of what you've allowed these packets to do to you. To your child.

And there it is again, with the painful release of air—the bark. There's no other way for it to come out.

These packets—whatever they are—have made you.

THERE WAS MAGICAL

THINKING AND THEN

THERE WAS—

GRASP

The smell stayed on my fingers all night, each moment that he wasn't coming home. Musk and forest floor. But not tiger.

Stop it, I told myself.

It's not coming back. It was never here.

It was only ever the smell of him disappearing.

At dawn I walked into the cold water, taking each step carefully so the broken shells, the barnacles that coated the big flat rocks, wouldn't cut too deeply into my feet. He was still not home. In my right hand, the machete. Agnes was back on the beach, charged with filling a basket with periwinkles. The *yellow* ones, I said. The water, I saw, was lapping at her feet; the tide was on its way back in, the slackness broken.

Back! I yelled. Go farther back!

I hacked through a strand of kelp the length of my body— the long blade of the knife slipping as I cut—and flung the broad, slick ribbon over my shoulder. Seawater soaked my shirt. I glanced back at the beach to make sure she was still okay. I bent and sliced again, flung the strand over my shoulder, felt the fresh soak of seawater, looked back to make sure she wasn't following. I should have put the life jacket on her. The kelp was a long wet beast. It held my blade, tried to strangle it.

No. The kelp was kelp. I didn't have to be such a fucking child. No tigers, no beasts.

•

The labels read:

Superfine Bali
120 grams
Not for Human Consumption

Sceletium-Cautauba Extract
28.8 grams
Not for Human Consumption

Enhanced Maeng Da
Extract Enhanced Premium Kratom
30 grams
Not for Human Consumption

Super Malaysian
Premium Powdered Kratom
60 grams
Not for Human Consumption

Oxindole Enhanced Bali
12 grams
Not for Human Consumption

Super Enhanced Indo
15 grams
Not for Human Consumption

I'd stared at the packages. I'd copied the words down on paper until they started to stick, until I could almost remember each syllable. Until they began to turn into something real. It was important to make reality real, however disappointing it was. I'd need these notes, too, when I went to do my research.

I hacked through another strand of kelp, freeing my blade.

I knelt and pulled my head under the shocking cold, keeping only my hand with the machete up and out of the water. The ribbons lifted off my shoulder and floated above my head. Agnes. I came up out of the water and turned to look for her.

She might come speak to me in the voice of an adult, I thought. She might flash her tail and be gone. So strange this new reality, governed by unknown hands. It was hard to know what to expect.

There was a slice on my knee and the blood was like a jellyfish in the water.

OTHER HAND

It was not a woman.

If it was this, it was not another woman.

The surf pulled back, rolled in, pulled back again. Pulling the strands of rockweed, predictably, along with it. Around my ankles. I was the woman.

I must have looked like an idiot there, grinning. Beaming out toward the sound. Draped in a sash of harvested weed. My hair tangled and salty.

A MINUTE MORE

It took twenty-two hours of waiting but there he was.

First the dory was just a speck, then I could make out its shape.

I wasn't ready.

I pulled Agnes through the ferns and kept on going, as far from the house as we could get. The tide was out, so at the point we kept on going, across the sand bar and up the jagged slate to the single oak tree, sidelit in the afternoon light. We sat among the spent shells—the bright orange plastic tubes (from rifles? shotguns?), bent and frayed, faded to white along their creases and cracks, in the abandoned duck blind, behind the curtain of stiff netting shot through with fragments of sun-hardened seaweed. My grandmother used to chase them off, the hunters—who were trespassing, maybe, depending on who you asked—but the blind kept coming back.

Some kind of flower grew from the cracks in the rocks.

Through a gap in the blind, we watched a family of ducks that didn't seem to mind where they were going.

Ducks, or loons.

God.

The unknowingness followed me everywhere.

ANOTHER MINUTE

Eiders.

I looked them up.

He'd been in the bathroom since we came back to the house.

The eider is the largest sea duck in the northern hemisphere.

It has a wingspan of forty-one inches.

It dives for mussels, clams, urchins, scallops, starfish, and crabs.

In winter, eiders spend half of daylight feeding.

Females pluck feathers from their chests to line the nests they make in grass.

I needed more information.

I took Agnes to the boat. The dead-man's clip dangled in place. I'd been a teenager when I last wrestled the engine, pulling the cord again and again until Conrad, or my dad, came and got it started. If it weren't for my grandmother, I might have thought that female bodies were just missing something. Some muscle in the shoulder that made the necessary motion possible.

He'd hear us leaving.

I felt for the car key in my pocket.

PLACE OF HIGHER LEARNING

Can I use a complooter, peas? I said, standing in front of the librarian. She handed me a guest pass, good for the sixty minutes. Thanks you, I said. She didn't bat an eye. Plenty of people must come at her like this. With questions forming mounds in their brains, interfering.

What I learned, with my complooter pass, was this: It's made from the leaves of trees in Southeast Asia. The stuff in the packets. This *kratom*, as it's known. *The leaves are chewed or drunk as a tea to elevate mood (as a euphoriant) and enhance physical endurance. As a medicine, kratom is used for anxiety, cough, depression, diabetes, diarrhea, high blood pressure, pain, to improve sexual performance, and to lessen symptoms of opiate withdrawal.*

I tried to see Paul in there. Which meant trying to remember Paul. But I was exhausted. Wrung out. Already trying to do more than I could handle.

Can you become addicted to kratom? I asked. It seemed no one else had thought to wonder; no one else needed to know. It was a stupid question, anyway. I just wanted to see, I guess, *how many* people shared this problem. How alone I was.

The retail sites bore disclaimers: *Goods purchased from the Seller are for herbarium specimen, for collection, for smudging, scientific research, and/or ornamental display. The Goods are not intended for human consumption under any circumstances. Any human consumption of the Goods is deemed misuse.*

What I wanted, then, very intensely, was to murder whoever wrote those words. To murder the courts and laws and lawyers that prop this behavior up.

It's illegal to purchase or consume, I notice, in the places where it's grown.

But perfectly legal here.

How to pronounce kratom, I typed. It would feel better, I thought—less silly—to know how to say the thing that brought us there.

But there's no consensus.

Kray-tum. Kra-tm.

Say it how you like.

Say it whatever way does not leave you feeling absurd.

It's $52.80 for three grams of *Oxindole Enhanced Bali.*

Sceletium-Cautauba Extract: $32 for five.

Here had been a turning point for me, at vet school: There was a broodmare in the school stable whose vulva gaped and had to be stitched to keep bacteria from finding their way into her uterus. This was not in itself unusual. Many of the mares had to be stitched; we learned how to open them up in time for the foal to be delivered safely, and then, after they'd had a few hours to rest—after we'd had a chance to examine the placenta for missing parts or discoloration and tend to the foal—to close her right back up. To stitch poorly was to put her at higher risk of infection than not stitching at all.

What set this mare apart was that for years she'd been with

another owner, one who'd used staples instead of needle and thread. This horse kept her hindquarters against the wall, her fear beating out any curiosity she might have had toward her baby. I stroked her neck and talked to her, sweating colder as each minute passed. I had to do this. I had to terrify her in order to save her life. The class was watching. Not even a vet school would keep a mare with a damaged uterus.

I couldn't do it. I couldn't get her into restraints. Couldn't get her tail wrapped. Couldn't get her cleaned up enough to warrant administering the local anesthetic. I left the stall, still telling her everything was okay.

That was my last day of vet school. Halfway into my third semester, on the heels of two years of equine studies. I just didn't go back.

The next student did it, I heard. Showed her he was in charge. Got it all done.

Okay, Mama? Agnes asked, parting the veil of hair to see my face.

I opened my eyes, to see her, in the bright sun.

The ospreys were up above, cruising. The air was cool. The sand was warm.

Paul must have known that something had changed. I'd moved the packets. Paul must have been riding out just a few more minutes, knowing what would come once Agnes was asleep. The dead-man's key was in my pocket.

SOCKETS

Do you love us?

His body was rigid. His arms crossed, fists ungodly tight. Was he going to spit?

You don't know anything.

I know *this*. The packets were laid out on the bedspread.

You don't know anything.

So tell me.

His face wrung itself tighter around his lips; the crimsons, blues, and purples rucked into a darkness like dried blood, the pinprick where they might come apart. The white scuzz of fear on the outer edges.

So tell me. Look at me. Tell me!

I wanted to claw the rings from under his eyes.

The ceramic lamp cast its glow from the low bench next to the bed.

I wanted to grab his eyeballs. Force them to take me in.

How much have you spent?

I don't know. Nothing. Hardly anything.

The lamp shattered, its shards skittering over the floor where it landed. I stood still, as frightened as Paul by what I'd done, waiting for Agnes to quiet—it was only sleep crying, some bad thing happening in the world of her dream. The glass of the bulb as fine as powder by Paul's feet.

The dark was better. His head was down. His shoulders rising and falling.

How much?

It's always about money with you!

Horrible wet sinews connected his top and bottom teeth.

How did it start?

All you cared about was Agnes! I was relegated to some fucking basement in your heart and I'm supposed to pretend it's okay. I'm fucking lonely.

No.

No?

My brain felt swollen.

You stopped coming home.

You barely looked at me!

When did you lose your job?

Oh right, the fucking money!

We were evicted, weren't we? And you were, what? Waiting for my grandmother to die? So we could come here and squat?

He was going to spit. The tightness couldn't hold.

The sinews.

This was for you, Tuck!

His face changed; slackened, like it was reverting to its natural state. In the darkness, I saw a desperate version of someone I knew.

What else could I give you? I want to be a good father. I want to be your husband. I want you to love me the way I love you. I'm so scared, Tuck. Tuck, I'm so scared.

•

What did you think would happen? I said this when neither of us had anything left. When we'd been lying on our backs in the dark for a very long time, and I'd done the fast sink toward the sea floor again and again. What did you think would happen to us out here?

He turned his head on the pillow to look at me.

I thought I'd get better.

Forgiveness, sometimes, beats itself free from behind closed curtains. Clumsy and sudden. With all the grace of an awakened pigeon, while the falcon watches on.

BACK

PROBLEM

It had made no sense to bring the lemon tree with us from Pittsburgh, and would have been impossible anyway.

It had seemed urgent, once, to get more. To turn the bedroom into an orchard of sorts, to stand the trees against the walls. They were cheery, for one thing, when healthy. The lemons so bright. But for another thing, I was accustomed to windbreaks, to the idea that trees hold together what's between them, keep it all from just blowing apart. The walls in the apartment were ugly: the paint an off-putting white with too much yellow in it, the grease stain from the last tenant's head hovering over the bed, the gash in the plaster near the door. The single lemon tree did its best.

Paul started taking the car to work, for reasons that remained unclear to me—he'd bicycled, before. Part of the problem was that I was protecting a secret, too. I was embarrassed: I'd spent all my own money, what I'd saved, on organic cotton blankets and whimsical outfits, wooden rattles and diapers that claimed to be more honest than others, as evidenced by the scree of cute pink giraffes that covered them. Honest? Diapers? Playmats and Boppies and a Jolly Jumper. Things I would start to sell off, for the supermarket diapers with Elmo on them.

•

I watched her hair grow. I watched her eyelashes grow. I watched her range of expressions—shadows of real thoughts passing behind her eyes—grow.

I didn't see *her* grow.

I didn't dare squeeze my nipples.

I was embarrassed by my hunger—for thinking of food so constantly. Surely other new mothers weren't like this. Paul did bring home what should have been enough, I thought. For a regular woman whose joy in love displaced her other needs, the selfish ones. I sorted the items into their places myself, so I would know what was there, sizing up the haul in terms of its relation to my body mass. How many times over, in a week, did one need to eat one's own weight? Once? Twice? Only half of it? A two-thousand-pound horse needs only four pounds of roughage per day. The rice would expand when cooked, of course. So would the noodles. Even the hard little lentils would grow.

When I stood up, I waited for the world to get still again, to come back into focus.

We'd never joined our bank accounts.

Finally, I did it. Asked if he'd leave me his debit card so I could take the bus to the Eagle. And he did. He left it with me—not the morning after I'd asked, because he forgot, but the next. I'd hoped he'd also leave me the car, but it didn't occur to him. I hadn't told him how stranded I felt, hoping he would just know it, instead. It was possible he was just exhausted: he was hardly ever home, his work was consuming him, there was Agnes. I couldn't get her to sleep apart from me, so she spent the nights in bed with us, up and down. He lay, in those days, with a pillow over his head.

We took the bus. I filled a cart and pushed it to the front of the store, where a woman with a doughy face and stringy hair rang me up. The card was declined. I asked her to take off the pineapple and the seitan and the jar of coconut oil and we tried again. We kept whittling it down. Never mind the bag of granola and the cottage cheese and the little box of yellow tomatoes. Goodbye, avocado. I think after so many tries, the woman said, it's just not gonna work. I think the bank puts a stop on it. Even if you got the money in there.

Okay, I said. I took a last look at the Enfamil on the conveyor belt. Maybe I didn't need it.

That's weird, Paul said. I'll have to call the bank.

We had a squash and half a bag of rice and some soy sauce and some pickles and some coffee and a quarter loaf of wheat bread and the peanut butter. Was that enough?

I ate some of everything. I squeezed my nipples. I looked.

We took two buses to the place where we got eight dollars for a few of the outfits she'd hardly worn, another five for the Boppy and some wooden toys.

The woman with the doughy face wasn't at the Eagle.

The instructions on the can said to check it for bulges, dents, or leaks. *If any of these are present*, it said, *DO NOT USE*. It said to get everything ready—to sterilize absolutely everything. To use only cold water from the tap, to avoid poisoning the infant with lead. To bring that water to boil and let it cool. Then to simply scoop, shake, and check the temperature against your own wrist.

Agnes had no qualms about taking the bottle.

She liked the ugly room in Pittsburgh—the city where I'd met a few of Paul's colleagues but no one else. She liked to be put on the blanket beneath the lemon tree after filling her belly. The light was dirty. I worried about the dust, the kind of dust that old apartments in old cities shed—the fine white powder that lands on countertops and windowsills and still surfaces of water, in more and more water glasses left by the bedside, because just staying home like this, doing nothing, was impossible to keep up with. You could clean up after yourself forever, the passing of time. I wiped the leaves with a damp cloth.

It was good to have my own hunger removed from the equation. To have it be a separate thing.

She lay on the blanket, looking up at the sunlight that came through the dense little leaves, and I compared her to the day before. On the record player, as it usually was at that time: a song about a lemon tree. An arrangement of calypso beats that infused our orb with sunshine and sweetness, with its 1960s innocence.

I had no desire to step out of our love: It was a physical space, an incredible wonder, a great relief to learn I was capable of inhabiting it. Outside of it, something was wrong.

•

It was the song Paul had hummed in the car, before I'd ever heard it. Before he bought me the record, then brought his record player over so we could listen in the sunlight of my big six-paned window, then started staying over so we could listen to more and more records he brought that I had never heard, confounding and exciting him.

The tree lay across the back seat of the car, propped up a bit—that posterior space, usually empty, turned into a little jungle of our making.

When the tree got mites right after I brought it home, to my rented farmhouse, it was Paul who did the research—Paul who picked off most of the leaves and put them, bagged, into the freezer before discarding them; Paul who took the straggly plant into the shower with him three mornings in a row; Paul who bought a dustbuster to vacuum the remaining leaves.

Paul who kept pots of water boiling on my stove to raise the humidity until the infestation passed.

Paul who rearranged my living room so the tree could be positioned where it had enough sun to relax.

The furniture was not my own, and it would not have occurred to me to move it. Soon we moved the sofa upstairs, and the bed down, so it could be by the big window, and by the tree. He liked getting up at dawn, awakened by the spreading light.

The books on the shelves were also not my own. He couldn't believe I hadn't read them. So he read them to me, aloud. *The Old Man and the Sea. The Collected Stories of Katherine Anne Porter.* Don't you see? he would say. Don't you see what's happening here? I tried to match his excitement. But I

didn't always see. It was enough to let it happen, on its own—
the unraveling toward an inevitably devastating end, without
my seeing the machinations of it.

Over the winter, *Anna Karenina*. Anna and Vronsky and Ob-
lonsky filling the cracks in our days. They had to, if we were
ever to finish. He started setting an alarm, for 6:00 a.m. Coffee, and foolish Kitty. And Levin: *Without knowing what I am
and why I'm here, it is impossible for me to live. And I cannot
know that, therefore I cannot live.* This overlay gave me a pleasing rush—Levin's words in Paul's voice. It was like getting two
men at once.

Don't you need to get to work? I said. He was still sitting in the
kitchen. Just sitting, head in his hands. He could have been
in the bedroom with us, all that time. Watching his daughter,
who was figuring out how to grasp a rattle and move it to her
mouth.

Before this, I watched him pull a newspaper out of his P.O.
Box. He never let anything drop—no ad sections ever slipped
out and got away. He was young to have a P.O. Box. Mostly, the
students used the mail center on campus. Even the ones here
for secondary degrees.

    Every Monday morning, I stuffed his box with Sunday's
Washington Post. I loved this about him a little bit right away:
his willingness to be a day behind.

•

He came toward my counter, the lobby empty. I'm sorry, he said, but someone has to see this. I looked him over—the eyes both dark and light, flecked, the hair cropped close to a nicely shaped cranium, the pen mark at the corner of his mouth— then read the headline he had placed in front of me: *Millennials fill their apartments—and the holes in their hearts—with plants.*

You disagree? I said, looking at him.

As a Gen-Xer, I'm embarrassed by all these public attempts to understand your set.

It's flattering, I said. Anyway, I'm an *older* millennial. The very oldest.

Once a week, I slid a thin FedEx SmartPost envelope with an Illinois address in the return field into his box.

Let's buy plants—a week later, scribbled on a scrap, inside the envelope with his monthly payment.

What hole is it you're aiming to fill today? I asked him, as he drove me along the road that twisted and narrowed on its way out of town.

Just a big one, he said.

I looked out my window so he wouldn't see my grin.

Our tiny months-old girl lay on the blanket beneath the tree, the edge of a tooth like a pearl behind her gum.

It must have been another woman. That was it. That was the problem that waited outside the space I shared with Agnes. The reason he was gone when I thought he should be home, the thing that made him inattentive to the needs I'd never learned to express, the thing that made it so nothing he said about time or money made sense. I could ignore it longer still. I could maybe even win this way, by growing an enormous love he'd want to step back into.

NOW

ROOMS

There are new rules, of course. Paul stays here. The boat is mine.

He shakes and shits and chatters as he withdraws. He stays hidden, mostly, not wanting an audience for this—though there are times, I think, when he turns up the volume on his suffering, wanting me to hear. Moments when he forgets that though he has little choice, he said he wanted this.

The internet says nothing about kratom withdrawal. But it says it's four to seven days for getting through the worst with other opioids.

I keep the dead-man's clip on my person.

Why not heroin? I'd said, in the morning, as I sorted dream from reality, when the only shards left were the ones hiding under the bed. He looked at me.

It must be cheaper, is all.

He looked at me again.

I didn't want to die, Tuck.

DRIVE

The executor will come by water taxi, I imagine. At unthinkable cost. His rental car—I see it as a black sports model, and he will have ridden with the top down, at least part of the way—will be parked in a flat lot in town at an exorbitant rate that will be charged against the estate. I listen for the sounds of an approaching boat.

Agnes doesn't want to leave the beach, but is being tender, cautious. Has been, since this new arrangement. We go to the kitchen, picking up the pillow and blanket from the grass on our way. We'll have to be able to slip into the trees undetected. I collect cups of water from the table, dry them, and put them in the cupboard. Where to put the damp towel? Already, I feel defeated.

On the floor, next to the stove, is the house we've built of playing cards, encircled by stones of Agnes's choosing. Only the top level has collapsed. Agnes was in awe of me—not jealous, for once, as she watched my steady, grown-up hands add card after card. I'd asked her if she wanted to blow it down when it was done. No, Mama, she'd said. We keep it. So we'd gone to the beach, to collect the stones, to give it berth. She's brought it other offerings, too: a clump of moss, a snakeskin, the tiny bone of a bird or fish. I kneel down and rebuild the top level, while Agnes watches.

Down the hallway, on the other side of the bedroom door, is Paul. When I get too close, I hear the steady expulsion of noise through his chattering teeth, not quite a cry, not a chant. Too meaningless to be anything like a prayer, though if I were standing with my feet on foreign soil, I might mistake it for one. The involuntary, relentless chatter of a fever, breaking apart, here and there, into higher scales, before collecting itself back into a low, steady stream.

Agnes is eyeing the door.

To the beach? I say. And we leave the cool, dim hallway for the bright sun, the dance of blinding water all the way east to the sound, come what may.

We find mussels, suddenly. Hordes of them, along the inlet where the vertical slats of slate cut into the water like blades. We gather them by the bucketful, lifting the heavy wet veils of weed from the rocks that are still dark from the wet of the receding tide, each uncovering accompanied by hope and curiosity and also some fear. Each time, as she clasps the fistfuls of pulled-back weed, she's quiet for a moment, her eyes taking in the dark pools between crags, the skim of grayish white larvae atop their surfaces suggesting another scale of life, the clusters of dusky shells clinging to black rock—the entire shape of things back there—before declaring her victory. Got some! she says.

The weeds just aren't enough. The bladder wrack and dulse and orache I've steamed with powdered garlic from the cupboard. We need more. We're looking at days of this. Days of this, and then—

My fingers ache, and sting; I lay my knife next to the mound of scraped-off barnacles next to where I sit. Up here, on the upper beach, crisp spiderwebs fill the gaps between the blades of rock, the silk brilliant in the sun.

Then: The sun's behind a cloud—a whole new sky of cloud—and I look away, too late, shivering off the slump of the webs, hanging there.

We bring water to boil in the huge aluminum pot.

After the mussels, I'll use it to boil our clothes.

Why you look like that, Mama? Agnes says, as the little animal—already dead, I remind myself—slides down my throat.

But already she's filling her mouth with another of the smooth globules, delighted enough to forget about me.

I saw a truck carrying cattle along our Indiana road when I was six, and haven't eaten an animal since. Hadn't.

I do him a favor and pretend to be asleep in front of the fire, where I've laid out the cushions I've plucked from the sofa, dense with the moisture of thirty years, spider eggs, and woodsmoke.

He wants to come out of his hole a new man. Having done this on his own.

When I can hear he's ceded the bedroom—when I hear the noise of him pass through the hallway and settle into the kitchen—I move in. Our silent arrangement.

·

In the morning, I notice the butterflies are gone. I wonder if they ever just die in midair, if the wind just slides right under them and carries them out to sea without missing a beat.

There's a white boat I've seen before, flitting from trap to trap in the glare of the sun, halfway out to the sound. Charon for butterflies, I decide. Because not everything we believe matters.

Still no hips.

Thank god that Agnes is sleeping. The sounds are more inside my skull than the croaks of the seals, and take me to darker, more horrible places. Some dread hands are twisting his femur for pleasure. Someone is showing him videos of his child being flayed. I pull the pillow over my head, squeeze it against my ears.

I wake up and the house is too quiet. He's gone. I run through the darkness to the dock, my light flashing on the roots ahead of me. Already he's coming back in. In the row boat. Sobbing. My light lights him up, and he lifts an arm to cover his eyes.

You can barely hold the fucking oars! I yell.

I watch him row himself the rest of the way in. He's nearly as white as the boat. I don't take my light off him.

He can barely get out of the boat on his own. His struggle is lit by my beam. Like a moth whose wings got wet.

But the moaning has stopped. I wonder if it's like a fever breaking.

In the morning I'll bring the oars to the mainland. So he can't try that again.

•

Again, she's dragged her blanket to the porch. We sip our pretend tea as I read to her from *Rumpelstiltskin*. The book is full of other horrifying tales of children being eaten or stolen, but she still insists on this one, again and again.

I like Rumpelstiltskin, she says.

You do? I say. What do you like about it?

Him, she says.

Once she's asleep, I drag the three big boxes out of the closet, untwist the garbage bags protecting the stock, and spread the kits on the floor.

Miraculously, they're not mildewed. I hold them, one after another, up to my nose to make sure. I do it again, disbelieving. They have an odor—they smell like this place—but it's not mildew.

I open one up and slide the contents out: the three rectangles of colored vinyl, the sheets of stick-on letters. My father had carefully researched proper letter ratios. I want to make sure they'll still stick on a bumper. I peel carefully.

W-H-A-T T-H-E F-U-C-K, I spell out.

My first bumper sticker in fourteen years.

When she's gotten her sleep, we'll go ashore. We'll turn these kits into food, and propane. I count them again, and again come up with 365. Like there are 365 of these islands. Like there are 365 days of this year, 157 of which are behind us, 120 of which remain to get off this island, allowing we're not discovered first.

•

Imagine if the executor comes when Agnes and I are gone, and finds only a sickly man cloistered in a bedroom; a child's boiled clothing hanging on a line. A card house on the kitchen floor surrounded by a sea of deep blue half shells, a countertop dirty with sea grit.

FREE YOURSELF

In Indiana, when I was fifteen, we moved the sofa into the garage and set up a long table in its place. The living room became a production room. Conrad—who was trusted more with the steel cutter—sliced the vinyl stickers to size from large sheets; it was my job to slide appealing color combinations into plastic sheaths, along with the appropriate number of stick-on letter sheets, and an instruction page that showed how wax paper could be used to configure your message before applying it permanently to the vinyl. *Careful!* the instructions warned. *The letters are designed to STICK through floods and ages.* Dad told me the adhesive was patented by NASA.

I folded a piece of card stock over the top of the sheath, stapled it on either side, and hole-punched it in the middle so it could hang on a rack in a store. Each time I reached for the supplies of card stock, I had to choose which message I wanted to present: *Free Yourself on the Freeway*, or *Express Yourself on the Expressway*. My dad couldn't decide which was better so he just didn't decide. His product had two taglines.

My preference then, as now, was *Free Yourself*.

•

Perhaps it's not so odd that they ended up here. The kits. That he lugged them over state after state, Indiana to here, to one of his mother's closets, the last time we came to visit her.

Throwing them out would have been a defeat he wasn't ready for.

Maybe he knew there'd be nothing left in Indiana by the time he came back.

DEAD STOCK

The motor starts on my twelfth yank of the cord. The sweat in my pits dries fast. It wasn't the labor. It was the alarm of absolute fucking ineffectiveness, baited to the surface with each useless, furious tug; each pitched, empty whirring of string ending in nothing. Some days are like this. But now there's a good low grumble, and the tiller's vibrating in my grasp. The sweat is dry, and the cool air raises bumps on my flesh.

Already I can tell I need to shit again. Agnes, at least, has been spared this—her stomach ready for anything, animal or not. The crabs we can catch on the beach are quick and delicate, babies. Her tiny fingers are suprisingly good at pulling off the flecks of clinging shell, after I crack them with a spoon. She's on the slats between my feet and the box.

It doesn't matter how I sit; my asshole is an itching, burning tangle.

It rained overnight and the day, at least, is sparkling and refreshed.

We cross the bay. We tie up the boat and climb the hill toward the Volvo, the box large enough to be awkward, but not so heavy I can't handle it. I keep Agnes under voice command. It's the same life jacket I wore at her age, even more mildewed now than it was then. If I didn't remember it as orange, would I see it as orange now? The stuff is more black than green. I'll take it off her when we get to the car. Flat straps of canvas, woven through rusted buckles, hold it on. Our butts are damp. Our clothing smells—I should have washed it ahead of the mussels. The bottom of the box, damp like us, is sagging. The burning is a driving force. I balance one edge of the box on the bumper, the other on my knee, while my hand flails around in my bag, searching for the keys. The center gives. The kits are in the mud.

It's okay, I start telling Agnes, who's screaming at the kits that aren't where they're supposed to be, while I pull down my pants and crouch in the brush. It's really fine. It's not a big deal to find something to wipe them off with. We can do it. There's no reason for us to act like this. I wipe my face with the back of my hand, to show her.

Soon Papa can help us, with something.

I look for anything to wipe my ass with.

There's the smell of coffee brewing and also the sharper smell of coffee roasting. I'm aware of the distance between my head and my stomach, which seems to be growing; the sensation is making me salivate. I can't tell if it's hunger or sickness. A channel between my right nostril and my sinus feels newly bored; it stings in a way that is at once shallow and deep; I feel it in my brain.

The woman offers me a cup of coffee and perhaps a cocoa, gesturing to Agnes, as we sit at a table with her forms. She has all kinds of knickknacks for sale—finger puppets, lobster candies, buoy ornaments carved out of wood. It's mayhem. I decline her offer because I'm not sure whether she means for free. I swallow and the saliva rises right back up. I keep my eyes on the consignment form.

If Agnes had any idea what cocoa was, there'd be hell to pay.

In the bathroom mirror, holding her, I look away. There's something about the sight of us here, set against these normal trappings—dark purple walls and small floating shelves holding up little fake plants—that causes me to panic. We look like something pasted in.

I wonder if that woman photographed by Dorothea Lange ever saw the picture.

Agnes is undisturbed.

Agnes is full of life.

And so I rally.

My stomach is officially empty.

On our way out, the woman catches us. Maybe she'd like a puppet? She takes two from the rack and holds them in front of Agnes. Which one do you like?

One is Ruth Bader Ginsburg, the other Einstein.

Agnes takes Ruth, and talks to it the rest of the day in hushed tones, so that I can hardly hear what she's saying.

ENTREPRENEUR

The bookshop at the other end of the strip mall took twelve and paid up front at $3.25 apiece.

The hardware store down the road said to come back when the owner was in.

The Jiffy Lube said they had to get permission from central management.

Still. Twelve times $3.25 is $39. Right here, in my hands.

TRIAD

We're imagining cheese sandwiches on thick, seedy bread, as we pull into the lot. We're imagining lumps of tofu that'll turn golden in the pan. Giant heads of broccoli to roast whole with garlic. We'll squirt lemon all over them when they're done, cut into them with knives and forks. Won't *that* be good, she says to Ruth. A couple of dark, juicy plums. Is it possible we could get one of those pizzas? I need to remember chickpeas. They can go in the pan with the broccoli. Or for later. Carrots are nice with chickpeas. I can shred the carrots, fry and smash the chickpeas, stir it all up with cumin and pepper. Zest it with the remaining lemon. And there we have our cheese sandwiches, much improved. Milk for Agnes, of course.

I know it can't all go to food, always. But for today, it will.

I check under the seats before we go in. What if a few extra coins are the difference between getting the pizza and not?

I stick my hand into the crack of the driver's seat—where the seat and the back of it meet. And there's something there. And though there's a quick flicker of hope, I can tell it's not money. Some signal from my animal brain tells my fingers to let go, but they don't.

They're receipts for money orders: $147, $82, $94, $132, $65. They're dated—one from each day of last week.

The burning is back in my gut and we beeline to the supermarket's toilets.

Everything he could get, I assume. However he got it.

My legs are asleep.

Instead of urging me along, Agnes, standing against the blue door of the stall, has just been whispering to the puppet.

Who's your new friend, I say, not showing that I hate it.

Rumpelstiltskin, she says. Then goes back to whispering.

The anger has to land somewhere.

MESSAGE

MICE

BE AN AGONIST!

I place each sticky white letter carefully on a piece of sky-blue vinyl.

The brain, the internet says, in its own way, is an overgrown wilderness—just a few goat trails make their way through. We, supposed commanders of these brains, are the goats.

A trail in Paul's brain goes the wrong way, is all. It's my job, now, to coax him in another direction. To be the sweet voice calling over dark thickets—a voice so full of the scent of clover that the creature there will look up, and tilt its head, and take a step into inhospitable terrain; my job to shake bags of grain, bleat seductively, get that goat to take a second step, then a third, in my direction, even as thorns slash into its flank, as burrs work their way deep into its fur.

I must project a land of plenty, of ease; a place with no past.

When he gets here, I must be the relief, the reward, the pleasure.

There's my face in the mirror.

Rumpelstiltskin? Agnes says.

She wants me to read it to her, is all. To her and the puppet.

What is it, exactly, you like about this story? I say to Agnes.

His magic.

•

Another day of this? Two? Until he's back?

We're starting to look a little more like businesswomen. We keep a comb in the glove compartment and pull it through our thin, fine hair after it's been whipped into strands on the boat. At the Goodwill, we each pick a new shirt to wear into the day. Agnes likes the smell of the chemical detergent lingering in the cloth. I'm happy for her, though it sears my nostrils and causes my head to thud.

The timing, really, isn't bad. The world is going to hell.

IT'S NOT THE TINY HANDS, IT'S THE TINY MIND. Turning left on a CRV.

GET HIM OUT! A Focus.

And on a bright red Ranger, pulling into a parking spot: WALLS ARE FOR GOOFBALLS.

I fought her last time, but this time I let her have it: the rotisserie chicken, spinning and hot, for $9.99.

On the hood of the car, where we dine, her face shines with the grease. I have no advice to give her on how to eat this bird, but she seems to know, preternaturally. I think just don't eat the bones, I say. But I can see the frustration rising. I can see what needs to be done. I grab the leg and pull, tearing ligaments and flesh, snapping bone. Here you go.

I should have grabbed more napkins. I have no choice but to lick the grease from my fingers, my palm.

What would Dad's say? His sticker, I mean. He'd have more

than this inchoate foreboding, this loose, ungathered sense of despair. He'd know his enemy—or at least have one chosen.

All who follow are lost. That one rode on the Dodge.

All who follow are complicit, he might say now.

But I need to keep these samples mild. I need money from everyone.

Dad would probably be in jail by now, if he were here. And I realize how true it is. How lucky it probably is that he lost himself somewhere else, before now.

ESCAPE YOUR TRAP BEFORE YOU'VE FASTENED THE LID.

One retailer's site linked to a study that demonstrated kratom's nonaddictive potential this way: A researcher fed morphine to mice then dropped them on a hot plate. After five days of this, the mice began to feel pain, requiring higher and higher doses of morphine. Those mice, when fed kratom leaves instead of morphine, still appeared to feel no pain after thirty days of being dropped onto the hot plate.

Okay, I think. But what happens on day thirty-*one*?

Okay, I think. But what if you drop *Paul* on that hot plate instead of a mouse?

And it's beside the point, but don't those mice *need* pain, I think. Isn't it bad for them to just stand there on that hot plate, grinning?

•

He hasn't come out of the room, and I don't hear his footsteps, so I crack the door, let my eyes adjust to the dark, and watch him. He's on the floor in the corner, hugging his knees, rocking. I can hear he's crying. He should die, I think. I bat it away, pretend I didn't think it.

In the morning, Agnes doesn't understand the rush, resists. The library opens at nine.

Kratom has been used safely by thousands to treat opioid withdrawal. Start now! What I'm trying to find out, late, frantically, is whether it's actually safe to withdraw from kratom cold turkey. Whether it's possible he *is* dying in there. Even alcohol withdrawal can kill you. Any good wife would have thought of this.

What I land on, finally, is a case study about a welder who fought his thoracic outlet pain with increasing amounts of oxycodone.

The patient reported successful self-management of his own oxycodone withdrawal by ingesting tea made from kratom, claiming substantial pain relief and increased social function. When economic pressures forced him to quit using kratom abrubtly, he experienced moderate opioid withdrawal symptoms that were unexceptional but for their protraction. Lacrimation was still profuse when he presented several weeks after onset of withdrawal symptoms—which he reported had included mild tremors, headache, mood swings, and rhinorrhea— for a single tonic-clonic seizure. Whether the event was attributable to his withdrawal was not determined. Toxicology was consistent with patient's denial of other substance use and CBC and BMP were unremarkable. Upon admission the patient was hypertensive and expressive of tachycardia. Patient responded well to amlodipine. The patient denied any previous history of seizures.

The study ended there as if anything had been determined. As if that information was useful to anyone. As if it gave me any clue as to why Paul was apparently the only one on god's green earth addicted to kratom alone. As if it told me what the fuck I was missing, and whether Paul would be okay.

I apply the letters carefully.
IN SICKNESS AND IN HEALTH.
I'll mess it all up if he learns of my thoughts.
What I want, more than anything—more than his health?—is a fat, tortured apology.
I put the sticker, with the others, in Agnes's sock drawer.

Agonista, it seems, is not a word. The internet suggested, instead, *agnostic.*

Some days the cool damp that emerges from the earth when I roll over a hollow trunk, hoping to show Agnes a salamander, does smell a little bit like my mother. If I'm honest. I should try harder to remember.

Some days you step out of the house and *whammo*, the smell of the ocean, of everything living within it, just wallops you. Some turn of the air.

Some days I play in the rain in the woods with Agnes and *whammo*, my need for the old Paul, for everything he used to be, staple-guns my heart against a nearby tree. Just, *thunk*. Some turn of the . . . what?

And then you either get used to the smell, or it goes away.

I'm busy, and my hands are full—gas jug and a plastic shopping bag containing three boxes of rice cereal (buy one get two free, a miracle). This one has to live in my head.

But the question, gathering force, starts to feel desperate.

At night, I put it down. Which does help, some.

DO YOU REMEMBER YOU?

I slide it beneath the mattress.

It's been ten days.

I wake up on the floor, in front of the fireplace. A few bright embers are nestled in the fresh gray ash, but that's it. The house is dark. I wrap myself in one of the blankets and sneak up the stairs to check on Agnes. I stop in the doorway. He's sitting in a chair he's pulled to her bed, his back to the door. I think, from the slump of him, that he must be asleep. Look how still he is. How at rest.

The heat takes me fast. What can I even do with that body, if he's dead?

I stare, without moving, until he gives a little sleep moan, a vocalized puff of nightmare.

I go to my room.

What now?

IN THE FARMHOUSE, FROM WHERE I SAT
READING A BOOK I HADN'T YET TOLD YOU
I WAS READING, MRS. DALLOWAY, I HEARD

YOU COMING DOWN THE GRAVEL, YOUR
WINDOWS OPEN, SINGING MAMMAS, DON'T
LET YOUR BABIES GROW UP TO BE

COWBOYS, AND YOU KEPT ON SINGING
AS YOU CAME IN, AND THEN SAID WOMAN,
WHAT'S FOR DINNER, AND I SHOOK MY HEAD,

AND YOU BROUGHT THE VEGAN POTPIE OUT
FROM BEHIND YOUR BACK, FROM THE BAKERY,
AND KEPT ON SINGING WHILE YOU GOT OUT

THE NICE CERAMIC PLATES AND LIT A CANDLE,
AND SAT ACROSS FROM ME, AND WAITED
FOR ME TO PUT THE BOOK DOWN, ONLY

HUMMING NOW, A RESPECTFUL VOLUME,
STILL GETTING THE TWANG IN THERE
THOUGH, AND THEN I PUT THE BOOK DOWN,

HAVING REACHED THE END OF A THOUGHT,
AND LOOKED UP, AND THERE IT ALL WAS, AND YOU,
QUIET NOW THAT YOU HAD MY ATTENTION,

AND GRINNING.

It's taken more than one sticker, of course. And I've had to steal from other sheets of letters.

I should probably stop wasting them. In case they really can get us out of here. In case they're our only hope.

In the mirror, I work on my face. Relief, pleasure, reward.

Training the muscles.

NATURE

To the south, the yellow-and-red ferry is crossing the bay to the populated islands—the islands with roads and electricity and ice cream shops and small art galleries for the tourists. The boat's a good two miles out, and won't be coming any closer.

Agnes and I count the starfish we see from the dock. At low tide, lately, we can spot them by the dozens, clinging to the underwater rocks. This is how it is here—species bloom, then disappear. There were hermit crabs by the thousands, in the shallows, only days ago. Now we can't find a single one.

Agnes wants me to pick a starfish up. I don't know how hard they can suck.

She won't let me get away with my fear.

Will it bite you, Mama?

What? No, baby.

Pick it up!

No, baby, I don't think—

Pick it up, pick it up, pick it up!

I plunge my arm into the shallow water, up to my shoulder, and peel one up, a little one. It's rougher than I expected, harder. I wait for the pain. I flatten my palm and feel its little suckers searching. I feel its otherworldliness. Agnes is delighted. I try not to show my fear.

Can I eat it, Mama?

I can't take it anymore; I throw it into the water.

Agnes erupts.

To the north hangs a dull fog, like a curtain, maybe thirty yards out. Coming through it now is the white boat I've seen before, attended by a flock of gulls, its lines strong but simple. Straight on, coming out of the pallor, the boat has a face: the two windows of the wheelhouse are the wide-open eyes, the orange life ring situated below them a little mouth of surprise. As it turns to sidle up along a buoy—brown, I can just barely see, with a yellow stripe—I see the form again. The curve of it in its orange slickers as it bends to the ropes, and hauls the trap over, that makes me look harder.

I'm sorry, I tell Agnes. That was bad of me.

Very bad, she corrects.

Each moment there's the possibility that another kit is selling.

YOUR KNOWLEDGE TEEMED
AT TIMES, UNREAL. YOU RAILED
AGAINST POLITICIANS, NAMING

THEM, AND THEIR ACTIONS,
LIKE THEY WERE PEOPLE I WAS
SUPPOSED TO KNOW. YOUR

KNOWLEDGE WAS THE ONLY
THING THAT SCARED ME THEN.
HOW DID YOU KNOW ALL THIS?

WHERE DID YOU KEEP IT?
IT WAS A PLACE INSIDE YOU
I COULDN'T GO. THE

INFORMATION ROOM.

At the library, I google *squatter's rights maine*.
   But no.
   To claim rights to a property here, you must first live in
it, or on it, for twenty years. You must show you've made
improvements.
   Back at the house, a breeze has disturbed our card house.
I set about rebuilding it, unprompted by Agnes, to whom I've
just given our last can of peach halves in juice. What remains:
a can of peas, a can of chickpeas, a slender sleeve of spaghetti
noodles. In the refrigerator, I know, are the last dregs of the
strawberry milk I caved on, half an apple baring its oxidized
face and arc of black seeds.
   What remains: our privacy, which is a relief. Since his night
at Agnes's bedside, he's tucked himself away again.

On the radio, reports of bad weather blowing in. A small craft
advisory. I'd like to listen longer—there's a story beginning
about a female Bhutanese falconer navigating the world of
IVF—but I unplug it from the wall. Diesel doesn't grow on trees.

•

I let Agnes do it. Into each of the six little burrows I've made with my fingers, she drops a single black seed from our apple. Together we push the soil back over them.

Why not?

Our basket—an imperfectly shaped thing woven from strips of reed dyed yellow and teal—is nearly full. We look for the shells that remain unblemished—no holes, no cracks, no mold, not too damp. This is difficult; these acorns spent the winter on the ground—and worse, the spring. Our plan is to crack them with a hammer and grind the meat into something like a flour.

A gust of wind pushes the upper branches of the trees toward the west. Agnes and I look up. Like most sky phenomena, it makes me feel like part of the world.

What that noise, Mama?

Wind, baby.

That.

I listen harder. The trees are groaning—sharp, creaking complaints. Now I see it's everywhere, on top of everything else: the threat of being crushed. From where we stand, I can see at least three thick birches straining.

Oh *that*, I say. That's the trees saying it's time to go inside.

Agnes doesn't want to go inside.

I drag her kicking and screaming.

Want to talk to the trees want to talk to the trees want to talk to the treeees.

Rain. Lots of it.

•

Inside the house, there is Paul. Sitting there, on the sofa. He looks bad—but better.

I'm sorry.

Did I hear it? It was nearly caught in his throat. The rain is loud.

I keep walking, cutting through to the kitchen, just as I'd planned, to light a fire in the stove. We're soaking wet.

It's fear, though. More than anger. Fear that my anger will make me do the wrong thing, and wreck him. Send him back.

While the kitchen fills with smoke, I try to unclench my jaw.

At least I know who won't appear, in this weather. The executor.

I'd looked for her first in the creek, sure she had drowned somewhere between its bursting banks. The roots of the slippery elms were exposed. If it hadn't happened, how could I see it so clearly? I entered the barn behind her and she didn't see me.

I watched as my mother braided the roan mare's mane. The gray mare was still in her stall. The roan mare chewed on hay while my mother gently brushed her white mane down along the side of her long neck with the soft brush. My mom was talking; I could make out the soft tone but not the words. The murmurs became harsher as she divided the mane into sections, tying each one off with a band. There was just enough edge in her voice, just in that fraction of a moment in which each band snapped into place, to sense that there was anger inside of her—not anger directed at the horse, just anger that was being released, slowly and quietly, almost inaudibly, as the horse chewed, not minding. My mother made fifteen sections, working her way down, then moved back to the top of the neck, behind the ears, and undid the band on the first section. Then her fingers divided the hair into three strands and worked them into a tight braid, which she tied off with plaiting cotton. She rolled the braid, hiding the end inside the coil, and stitched the bob off with the cotton. She did this fifteen times, working her way back down the mane. Then she did the forelock. She stepped back to assess her work. If the horse hadn't been old and useless, just the way she was when we took her in, the way both of them were, she'd be ready for show. My mother undid her work, snipping the cotton string from each coil, gently sliding her fingers through each braid to work it out, combing, combing.

After she left—left *us*, I mean—I found Conrad weeping. He was twelve. Who will love us? he said. *Dad,* I blurted, almost angry. But I regretted it right away. Regretted not asking him what he felt was gone, what he perceived as our mother's love. Did she have a way of running her fingers through his curly hair? A secret wink across the dinner table? And I'm left with this doubt. Was she broken, or was I? What had I missed?

But I didn't ask. His need to believe he was loved, or had been, made me more protective of him, in the years that followed.

Does he still feel it? Is it easier for him, in whatever shell-shocked desert he inhabits, to feel loved, or unloved?

Kray-tum, I think. *Kra-tm.*
    We're out of propane.
    I need the rain to stop; I can't go ashore in this.
    We did go out, Agnes and I, pulling back fistful after fistful of rockweed, to no avail. Like the mussels were only ever a dream.
    I let the remainder of the spaghetti noodles slide into the pot. A forty-nine-cent meal. I add half the can of peas, bring it up to ninety-eight cents, wondering how much I'll regret it.

I've given up on keeping a fire. Our skin and hair and clothes hold the water anyway; sitting next to the stove, Agnes had steamed. To get warm, we bury ourselves together in blankets. Agnes and I. Paul hasn't yet tried again. Emerging. Apologizing.
    If I were kinder, I think, I would go to him.
    I've discovered a canister in a low cabinet, behind the mess of my grandmother's pans and dented measuring cups, her old crank sifter with its wire mesh that's clogged with hard white sediment. The rice might have been in there five, ten, fifteen years. No telling. I reach my hand into the canister, feeling for unwanted objects as the grains filter through my fingers.
    I saw a mare—not our own; this was later—relieved from her misery. The fur on her muzzle worn away by her violent

rubbing of her head against the wall of her stall. I was shown the moldy corn behind her incurable illness, and slides of the liquefaction of the white matter of her brain. Lakes where fields should be.

My hand is coated in a fine white powder. I beckon Agnes over. She stands before me and I spread out my fingers. I press my hand against the damp blue sweater over her belly, and pull it back to let her see the print I've left against the blue.

Want to do it, she says, as I knew she would.

I let her put her own hand into the rice, and she puts her mark on me.

My grandmother drummed her fingers on my head like rain.

There's a gap in the rain. A slackening in the wind.

We go.

Ashore, we drive north with the bumper sticker kits, looking for more places to sell them. There's a running, impossible calculus in my head. Each mile traveled is gas spent.

After I got my driver's license it was my job to rove the state on Saturdays, looking for new stores willing to carry the kits. I passed through unfamiliar towns, noticing places I could try to make a pitch: card shops and drugstores, pawn shops, auto garages.

Mom might have been inside any of those places.

I never got out of the car, even to use a bathroom.

It would be better anyway, I thought, if Dad got a job.

We were only afloat at all, I suspected, because of help from my grandmother.

An antique store, a flooring dealer, a pizzeria. A florist? I swing the Volvo into the lot, gravel crunching under our wheels. The sign says they'll be open at eleven. It's ten till, now. I lean toward the glove box and feel around for the comb.

At the back of the fields behind the Indiana house was a tractor, its skinny back wheels half sunk into what would have been the creek bank before the creek meandered ten yards the other way on its route to the Ohio.

I must have been nine.

I'd climbed up on the cracked leather seat of the tractor. It burned the flesh between my legs; the sun was high and hot.

You're fine, my mother said. Her eyes scanned the tree line.

I wanted to show her that it didn't hurt. The fact she didn't attend to my pain. I grabbed the wheel.

Woo-wee, I yelled, thrashing my hips forward and back. We've got ourselves a buckin' bronco!

Shhh, she said.

I watched her listen to the blanket of noise that was Indiana summer, her eyes still on the trees. The buzzing of insects and the chatter of birds that you didn't hear until you did, and then it became overwhelming, how not alone you were.

She started back to the house.

Before that, I was not allowed to play on the tractor alone.

There was a lot of rusty metal, the brittle, perforated back of the seat a razor. But she didn't say come, so I didn't follow. When she was halfway across the field, I began to ride my bronco again, first silently, then with rising glee.

Agnes has been on the porch flipping the pages of a book she's taken off the shelf. The Book of Common Prayer. Inside, on a bookmark inscribed by my grandmother's hand: *For God alone my soul in silence waits.*

Of all things to be hurt by.

Meandered, I think, is the only word that's used when a creek goes off course. It's so jolly.

Our marriage has *meandered*, I decide to think. I decide to think like this for the day.

And it's nice, I admit. There's a lightness to my thoughts.

La-diddy-da-diddy-da-diddy-do.

As my grandmother used to say.

What do you put aside when you decide to believe in something?

Does it matter more for a thing to be correct, or useful?

I'm sprawled on a beanbag in the children's section of the library with Agnes, reading a book she's picked from the stacks. A warty troll has stolen a little boy's cap, which seems to

possess some magical properties. What is it with this girl and
her troll-like guys? Agnes keeps her finger on the page so I
can't turn it. The little boy looks so distraught. When I try to
turn the page she actually screams.

On the computer, I google: *Can you apply for public assistance if your address is a private island?*

I get no real answer, of course. But I do see other people's
related questions: Does welfare come to your house? Can I apply for food stamps without my husband? Can you go to jail
for using someone else's food stamp card? Can I live with my
boyfriend and still get food stamps?

And yes: They can and do, sometimes, come to your house.

I know the answer to my own question, of course: Not with
a straight face. Not without dying first of shame. Not without
looking into the eyes of each person you've just cut ahead of
in line.

I google also, for good measure: *Can you apply for public assistance if you've just been a fucking idiot, and blind?*

As an answer, this time, the internet offers Tucker Carl-
son's Wikipedia page.

I scan it, just in case.

Bastard.

When I'd come back across the field from the tractor and we'd
eaten our supper, I was washing the dishes at the kitchen sink
and became aware of my mother's presence in the doorway of
the adjacent room, my father's study. She leaned against the

doorframe, her back to the kitchen, her right foot crossed be-hind her left. She was wearing a blue wraparound skirt that hit midcalf.

I heard whip-poor-wills today, she told him. At noon.

I wasn't sure of what, exactly, she was accusing him.

I couldn't hear what my father said, over the running water, which I didn't turn off. He was back in the closet, I thought, looking for whatever he'd been looking for all day, despite the smell from whatever had died in the wall back there. A pos-sum or a squirrel.

Because it doesn't make any sense, she said. Because I want you to know that I'm surrounded by things that don't make sense.

I turned to the sink again, but I could tell when she was gone.

Mom's exacerbation started behaving on certain days like a flock of dark birds—rising suddenly. She stayed in the barn more and more, where a certain logic must have ruled her days. We didn't disturb her. We knew our incoming would be like a rock hurled into the mass of feathered bodies.

The line at check cashing, at the supermarket in the city, has been at a standstill for a while now. They should have another teller.

The other stores give me cash up front, but not the coffee shop woman—she does consignment, and pays with checks. She bought one of the kits herself though, it appears, and put

the sticker on the back of her brand-new Prius: COFFEE WILL
SAVE US.

I took the check from her hand.

She's expanding into wholesale and wants a delivery girl.
She put her hand on top of Agnes's head and I imagined swal-
lowing rocks—big, smooth rocks that I could just get down.

You can put this one in day care. I bet she'd like some friends.

A nice round hunk of granite.

Things look bad further down, the man behind me says.

Whatever else you might say about him, he's maintained
the perfect distance. He's mastered the art of personal space.

I crane my neck to look, but know he doesn't mean farther
down the line. He means farther down the coast. The storm,
this new one, is on the news because it's the third, I think,
for those who are drawing distinctions. And so early. An odd
year, or the end times, depending upon your camp. Depending
upon your state of mind. He has long hair, part of it braided.
He has dirty fingernails. I like his voice.

I was in a storm like that, down outside Tampa. Woke up
in the barn and went outside. The other barns were shredded
and the horses were dead all over the fields, some of them. Gift
for sleeping heavy.

I've seen dead horses, I say.

Not that I'm from Florida, he says. Wouldn't be from there.

I've seen them die.

He starts to whistle.

What he's not going to get to know, because I've stopped
liking him, is anything else.

The whistling is starting to bother people. The woman behind him is getting properly agitated.

Finally I'm at the front and I can set Agnes, who's gotten heavy, on the counter. Sometimes, these days, she refuses to be held, and sometimes she refuses to be put down. She always gets her way.

Beginning of the month, the teller says. Unemployment checks.

So look at us. Fancy enough to get this apology. White enough, I guess, and not obese.

With my hands free of Agnes, I'm able to dig around in my bag for the check. I slide it across the counter, and claim my $22.55.

I buckle her straps and kiss her forehead.

What, Mama? What that face?

And it is so funny. Explaining my face to her, so often.

It's my *face*, I tell her, poking her rib. I'm not sure what I can tell you.

We're gassing up with the money. There's one of our stickers on the Crosstrek in front of us: UNSTABLE ATOMS OUT OF THE HANDS OF UNSTABLE MEN.

When I check the pump it's reached $12.02—$3.02 more than I'd planned to spend.

Agnes is asleep.

The bell jangles as I push through the door.

Can I return gas? I say.

But I slide twelve dollar bills and two pennies across to the attendant.

Behind her, next to the condoms and the trucker speed and the ibuprofen, is a row of square black boxes, each boasting a big red K. I look more closely. *Super K*, the packages say. *Kratom blend.*

Popular? I say, nodding at them while a heat sears my heart.

Most people go with ribbed.

No, I say. I meant the—

But what does it matter.

We're all alone, or we aren't. Besides, this stuff looks cheap. Harmless. It's $11.99 for the box. Child's play.

Which doesn't mean I leave uplifted, hopeful, ready for whatever challenges the real world, our eventual return to it, may bring.

He'll have to go ashore soon, I know. I'm not thinking these kits are our answer. After the gas, we have $10.53 for food.

That was pride, I realize. Back at the gas station. Pride that whatever *my* husband had been taking was more powerful than whatever was inside those square black boxes. Which were for chumps, most likely.

I do and I do not want to know how he got the money. What he did. What I would have to do, if I knew.

GIFT

The sound of the metal crank, as it made its way through his bone, must reassert itself in his head, sometimes. He gave his marrow to a stranger, once. Simply because he learned that he could.

Maybe he's been selling plasma?

Agnes and I stop by the bookstore, and while we wait for the manager to get back from lunch, we browse. In the local section, I find a book on foraging in the woods of New England. It's large and hardcover and full of beautiful color photographs on thick paper. I check the price. The clerk has come near to shelve new stock.

Right on, he says, seeing what I've got.

A bit much, though, I say.

He guides me to the disorderly used section—this place is buy, sell, trade.

Pleased with himself, he extracts for me a slim, yellowed pamphlet from 1976. Inside are simple line drawings of various plants, and a disclaimer that no book of this sort is meant to be authoritative.

There's a price penciled in on the upper corner: $3.50. It feels like a wise investment. The manager comes out, seems happy to see me, then frowns. Things'll pick up in a week or so, she tells me. When the summer people start to arrive. Meaning no kits have sold. She makes me take the pamphlet on credit—a sign of her faith, she says.

It's funny: There are people we can accept things from, and others we can't. With this woman, I don't sense any scheming. I suspect she'll forget this kindness as soon as I've walked out of the store.

The boat ride back is bouncy, but we make it without a hitch.

Agnes and I check our acorns, which are still spread across the kitchen table. It was ridiculous of me to think that anything could dry in this house.

Still, we take them onto the porch, and have a good time smashing them to bits with a hammer. Paul steps out to watch us from the other end of the porch. I let him watch but don't acknowledge him.

If he spent $490 in five days while we were here, how much has he spent over the course of Agnes's life?

We pick out the fragments of shells and assess what's left.

I notice that he's gone.

The flour, objectively speaking, is a disaster.

Still, I mix it with a little water, roll it out, and fry it up.

There's nothing tentative about Agnes's approach. She eats until there's nothing left.

There must have been a time, though. At some point. When

Paul was Paul. Some timelines of human evolution show you the bodies—slumped, then rising. Some show the skulls.

Those weekly envelopes from FedEx SmartPost I slipped into his box. There are some things I don't have to wait for him to confirm for me.

Motherhood suits you, he said, finding me pinned to the sofa by my enormous stomach, my ankles the shape of tin cans, the bucket and mop abandoned in the middle of the floor.

It was beautiful, the way he picked up where I left off. The way he slid right in, revived the mop, and took over. Moved aside the chairs I would have just worked around. So beautiful, I barely even noticed the change. The quick, discreet departure of my autonomy. It was as good as the floor in that apartment had ever looked. The old wood uneven, but gleaming.

Now it's as shiny as you, he said.

At night, I work it out on a piece of stationery from my grand-mother's writing desk. It takes both sides of the sheet. Agnes is 902 days old. It's a mess of columns—problems of multiplication converted into neighborhoods of towers to add up. But if we extrapolate a $98 daily average from his last week of using, and multiply that by 902 days—

$88,396.

Agnes ate half the packages of instant oatmeal in six hours.

The wind is too strong to go ashore.

He puts his hands on my shoulders, from behind, and I sit like a stone.

The impatience is a sudden shrill shrieking in my skull. I can't do this. We're still stuck out here. I know exactly where they are, but Agnes won't lie down. I pull my hand back so it won't shove her head down against her pillow and hold it there. I clasp my hands behind my back and take a breath. It's probably her hunger keeping her from settling down. It's probably mine, which I know she also feels—we double the feeling by knowing each other too much. I close my eyes and try to let the shrieking drain out, try to let it be replaced by the outside shrieking of Agnes.

Let him see us like this.

I take a breath. I walk out the door. She'll wear herself out and fall asleep, I know. I just want her to do it quickly. She's wasting calories on this.

I snap the batteries out of the kitchen radio and drop them back into my flashlight. They bounce against the springs and settle into place. I stand on tiptoe and with the tips of my fingers coax my grandmother's cherrywood bowl from the top of the cabinet and head out into the dark, my beam picking up the sideways rain that strikes my cheek. We'd seen them earlier. Our rule is no mushrooms, but everyone knows you can eat chanterelles. I cast my beam about until it lights up the orange profusion.

I fill my bowl. It's a solid, well-made thing, and it feels good between my stomach and the crook of my arm.

In the kitchen, wet and hungry, I stand still and listen. She

must be asleep. The pain is swift and sharp: There are more
and more of these moments when she's better off without me,
the disturbances I bring. I spread the mushrooms on the table
beneath the hanging bulb, bright caps down, ridged under-
sides up. The glowing stems stretch upward toward the ceiling.
Drops of water slide down the ridges and pool at the pale furls
along the edges of the caps. I look at them.

You are chanterelles, right? I say.

My pamphlet intentionally does not deal with mushrooms.

But the little paperback field guide from my grandmother's
shelf is opened to the correct page, facedown, on the table.
They are, as far as I can possibly tell, chanterelles.

There's still a little of my grandmother's lard left in the
ceramic jar next to the stove. I put a small amount into her
heavy cast-iron pan and leave it to warm while I slide a knife
through a single mushroom, slicing it into thin slivers. I drop
the slivers into the pan and let the heat and lard move into
them, make them even more tender. My mouth is filled with
saliva and a nauseating hunger is rising up from the pit of me.

I eat the pieces out of the pan, as slowly as I can. I want
more. I want more even if it will kill me.

But I sit at the table, with the uncooked mushrooms spread
before me, the heat off under the pan, until morning. If I'm
still fine then, I'll cut the remaining mushrooms into unrecog-
nizable bits and fry them up for breakfast for Agnes and me.
I'll serve them with what's left of the rice. Then we'll have a
little more for lunch. And a little more for dinner.

When I wake up his fingers are on the curve of my back.
A horse caught in a field. Picked up by hurricane winds and

dropped down here, the others all dead. Lying on their sides. Its eyes, I know, are far from still.

Tuck—

This isn't meandering, I say. *Meandering* isn't accurate here.

EXPLANATIONS

DRIVEN

I was dreaming about assembling the kits—my hand couldn't make the hole-puncher work—when Mom did it. When she left. In the morning, even the mares were gone.

Dad used the landline in the other room. All day he was on the phone. I could hear his voice: frantic, aggrieved, accusing. I continued my work: periwinkle, magenta, saffron, *staple*; vermilion, charcoal, aqua, *staple*.

She hadn't left a note.

Years later, Conrad told me he woke up that night, and she was watching him. Just sitting on the end of his bed, looking at him. And she told him to go back to sleep, and he did.

After the rest of us were gone, Conrad stayed in the house long enough to watch the crews lay down roads, first tearing up the trees, the fortress of raspberry bushes, then dumping and smoothing the gravel. When it was time for the house to come down—sold, by its owner, to one of the developers—he packed what he needed into the 4Runner he'd earned from dropping out of high school and working cash jobs for people he knew, and drove, first, to Lincoln, Nebraska, to visit the Museum of American Speed. When he landed in Mendocino County and wouldn't say exactly what he was doing, I figured he'd set up a good life growing weed. The next time I heard from him, he was already training at Fort Hood in Killeen, Texas.

Dad had gotten a degree in chemical engineering. He'd moved with my mom to Birdseye in the early eighties, mostly, it now seems, to avoid getting work. To build a utopia on a piece of old farmland. To not join the pharmaceutical industry. To not work for the military.

Dad was the one against a TV in the house. I don't want you all turning out like everyone else, he argued, every time we begged. You're *better* than that. Mom stood with him at first, but her allegiance seemed to flag over the years. I suspected, sometimes, when I found her sitting upright at the edge of their bed, staring at nothing, that a television might have been a welcome distraction.

What would have been different if we'd had one? What understandings might I have of the world? I consider the ease it might have granted.

PASSAGE

It was a passage I read in a book when I was very young. I can't remember what exactly else was happening in my life at the time, but young James Herriot's arms up inside a cow on a frigid winter night became the coziest thing I had ever known. It became my vision of warmth.

ONWARD

ADVISE

Albeit: a word I don't use often enough.
    THE FLOUR IS MEALY, ALBEIT EDIBLE
    THE MOUSE POPULATION IS SMALL, ALBEIT GROWING
    THE MOUSE POPULATION GETS INTO THE DRIED MILK,
ALBEIT NOT FOR THEM
    TIME IS SWEET, ALBEIT DESTROYING
    THIS GIRL IS TOO SMART, ALBEHER DEPRIVED OF OPTI-
MAL SUSTENANCE
    THE DAYS ARE TOO LONG, ALBETHEM TOO SHORT
    Finished, Mama? Agnes asks, reminding me of why I'm sit-
ting here, all this vinyl spread across the kitchen floor around
me. I'm so, so bad at this. I'm the worst bumper sticker kit
entrepreneur there could ever be. Still.
    YOUR MARRIAGE IS AWAY AT SEA, ALBEIT A _____ SEA
    YOUR ONLY HOPE IS TO SELL ALL THESE FUCKING
THINGS, ALBEIT
    Feed your hope again, albeit missing. Leave the bread out.
Put the sugar bowl on the floor. Let him come.

I consider turning the radio on, but talk myself out of it. I can
see well enough it's still raining.
    Lobsters live deep, Agnes says.

That might work, I say.

I move Agnes off my lap and get up out of the rocking chair, put the field guide on the table. I've been watching the tops of the trees, and am relieved by their dance. It's not that they're staying still, it's that I can tell, from second to second, which way they're going to blow.

I press white letters against a red background.

LOBSTERS LIVE DEEP LIVES

She's proud of herself, but god, kill me, she's trying not to show it. I've never seen that particular smile. I could eat her.

I open the junk drawer next to the refrigerator—full of scraps of charred tinfoil and the thick rubber bands used to hold shut lobster claws—and look down at the Sharpie my grandmother used to label the various jugs and cans in the shed, and I'm tempted to do it. To write our names on our arms. *A is for Agnes*, I would start. It would make her laugh. The cool touch of the felt against her flesh.

I wonder if he'll be well enough to get a job. If I can trust him to go ashore. One hundred and five days, starting here. That's what we've got. An eternity. Nothing. Until we have to be gone.

For now, of course, the wind works its own plans. The wind keeps us all right where we are.

Help yourself, I say. By all means.

Agnes and I are slurping at bladder wrack broth. We caught

four baby crabs so their meat is in there, too, somewhere. He's standing at the edge of the kitchen.

You have to eat.

He doesn't move, so I put my bowl down and get up. I get a new bowl and pour some off from the pot.

Take it to your room if you'd like.

I'd be embarrassed to eat, too.

We take a chance. We seize a moment of relative calm. We climb into the dory.

The calm, of course, was a fool's calm—calm within the shelter of the rock, but not beyond. This optimism has gotten me here before. A few times a minute, a great slosh of roiling bay comes in over the edge of the boat—we're low to the water, and it doesn't take much. Agnes loves it. Hold on, please, though, I tell her. That life vest. We'll test it, I think. When the sun's out next, we'll swim from the dock, in good, deep water. Cold as it may be. It's time. I go through the mechanics of it again in my head—what I will do if this motor gives. I'll crouch my way to the bow. I'll lay my stomach over the front bench and get my arms around the vast coil of thick, wet, salty rope, curled up there like a giant sleeping constrictor. I'll toss over the anchor at its end and let the rope slide through my hands until I feel it slacken. And then, because I don't really know what I'm doing, I'll give it the rest of the line, as well. So we won't be dragged to sea, or dragged under.

Off our starboard side, I notice the white boat with the face. I notice that the lone figure, in orange, is noticing us, too, on this uncouth water. I see that Agnes has just taken a spray in the face, and is drenched. I see that she's perhaps the happiest I've ever seen her—that she's unaware of anything outside the pleasure of it, the excitement of riding the back of something utterly uncontrolled.

I see, in the brief moment we're both able to take our eyes off our tasks, that the person seeing me, from within the orange slickers, is a woman.

I see that her dark hair is cropped near her chin and doesn't get in the way of her face—which mimics, for a second, the face of her boat. The O of the mouth. A slackened slate at total odds with the work of her body.

How pleasing.

Yes, this is us.

I T-bone the dock and dive to the bow to get a rope around a cleat, while the wind swings our stern. I abandon hope and scramble back to my bench, nearly tripping over Agnes, grab the throttle, and start again, making a wide circle into the restless harbor. I see my hand is bleeding from the palm. I come at the dock again and this time I manage to get myself onto the wood and plant my feet and keep hold of the ropes—keep the ocean and wind from tearing the boat and Agnes away.

Stay *down*, I yell.

The other boat is gone.

At the library, no one has seen a thing—how I have or have not endangered my child. Maybe the wind whipped up my recklessness. Maybe my victory made me bold.

Mr. Pettengill,

It might be worth asking what will happen with the is-
land property if my father isn't located. I assume my
brother and I are his next of kin. Please advise.

I'm not sure I want to know the answer. But I've hit send,
and there's no going back.

Maybe I'm just out of options.

The person who was here before me left a book on the table:
God and Vitamins: How Exercise, Diet and Faith Can Change
Your Life. The search history shows that the last two searches
were for: *Are vitamins real?* and *Does God work?*

We sit and watch the rose seller from a distance. The market
sets up across from the library, and I like these days best. She's
eighty, easy, her thick legs wrapped in knitted stockings, even
now. Last week, she had me carry a basket of her brochures
that had been peed on by a tall poodle to the trash bin across
the square; she'd first pulled a few out from the bottom of the
stack. They'll dry, she'd said.

More wind sneaks up the channels between buildings and
knocks over three of her bushes at once. We watch her flag
down a girl to set them right.

The other farmers are gone or packing up—their vegeta-
bles and jars of honey and racks of eggs and slabs of bloody
meat loaded into the backs of their trucks.

We should get going, I say.

She's like a bivalve, I add. She sits and waits.

Agnes beams when we step onto the crosswalk and all sorts of hair whips my face—hers and mine—and I can't see and I'm afraid we'll be hit by a car.

I watch in awe as a woman drives her car once, twice, three times into a telephone pole. Smash, reverse; smash, reverse; smash. I can't quite see her face.

I do know it's too dangerous to cross.

There's a dead fox on the side of the road and for a moment I watch its red-gold fur being pushed to one side, blowing like grain across a field.

Our Indiana neighbors always pulled a double crop—wheat then soybeans—which stressed my mother out but meant the registration tags on their cars were always up-to-date. We weren't farmers. We were just there—resisting capitalism, the prevailing culture, viable employment, honest conversation among ourselves—until we weren't.

At the supermarket, we use our $6.32 to buy Saltines and a new twelve-ounce jar of Skippy. We eat them in the parking lot, getting the peanut butter on our hands as we dip the crackers into the mouth of the jar. The peanut butter gets in our hair. I watch the coffee shop woman leave her store across the lot—the wind blowing her linen pants against her legs and revealing their shape—and then get into her Prius. We wipe our mouths with our arms then rub our arms with our fingers until the peanut butter gathers into tiny balls along our hairs. We go into the Goodwill so Agnes can play with the toys. We turn our remaining dollar into a blanket.

At the water, we shove the boxes of kits aside and fold the back seats down. The blanket is homemade—a sheet of sky-blue fleece pocked with yellow, cyclopean alien sorts. Wielding tools, wearing overalls. The edges of the blanket are cut and tied into fringe. The canopy, oaks mostly, heaves above us. The wind shakes the car. My body is spooning Agnes's.

He can worry about us, for a change.

FIND THE BEAUTY IN IT, said one of the stickers I'd seen in town.

It's a *leaf*, I find myself saying, laughing, sitting up in my sleep. It takes me a moment to remember where I am. I've taken most of the blanket, I see, and I return half to Agnes.

I read, once, in reports of a major power outage during a winter storm, of a mother and father who put all their children in a bed together for the night, their electric boiler being down, and thinking the children would keep one another warm. In the morning, they found their three older children wrapped and sleeping, breathing quietly, and the littlest one, alone on a bare corner of the mattress, frozen dead, his tiny knees drawn up to his chest.

I give all the blanket to Agnes.

The branches above us are still. The broad leaves filter the spreading light. It's day fourteen of this. Of Paul, on the island.

June is nearly behind us. Welcome back, I say, when she opens her eyes. Subduing my joy at having her with me for another day. But she feels it. We head down the hill. The dory has made it through just fine.

SPOON

It's no longer the island of my grandmother's house. It's the island of eelgrass and jackknife clams, waved whelks and dead-man's-fingers. Of bull thistle, nightshade, and hawkweed. Of sheets of pearly everlasting. It's the island of sugar kelp, soft sourweed, and of course the waving beds of purple dulse. When we're ahead of the gulls, it's the island of Aristotle's lanterns pried from the mouths of washed-up urchins with the stink still on them. These are the urchins that died free enough to be carried by the tides, the ones that did not use their teeth to scrape out little burrows for themselves in rock and coral, the ones that did not grow too large inside these burrows to move again. The ones that were not tucked in for their deaths.

I wonder if my grandmother read the books on her shelf the way that I do now. If to her this island was never hers, but the home of a thousand clamoring species, the names of which rattled through her brain. I wonder if this was the drama that sustained her, the contents of the inner life that showed itself only as the quiet smile, the mask of a hum.

La-diddy-da-diddy-da-diddy-do.

It was dusk, and she led me by the hand deep into the ferns, to show me where the spring bubbled up into a little marsh, the frog eggs attached to the underbellies of wide blades of

pale grass. These frogs can only live right here, she said. I remember the rustling through the undergrowth, the long low
gronk moving with the ferns, my grandmother giving my
hand a gentle squeeze and saying, only, Buttermunk. I wasn't
sure where this new endearment came from, whether she had
me mixed up with someone else, if there was something I was
supposed to understand. I held her hand and kept silent, to
mask my confusion.

As a child, here, I could lie awake in the silence, or I could slide
out from beneath the heavy blankets and creep down the dark
steps and into the blackness of the trees. I could lose myself in
the darkness, and still know I wasn't lost; the ocean hemmed
us in. It was just a matter of time before I found my way back
to the house, stepping carefully so as not to get hurt, placing
my hands against the trunks of trees, one and then another,
feeling my way through, then climbed the dark stairs back to
my bed with my hands on the top of each step, and finally fell
asleep.

I could do that once each summer, in the beginning, while
everyone else slept or tried to sleep in the different kind of
quiet, and stillness, and for the week that followed I could fall
asleep as soon as my head hit the pillow, just after I'd blown
out my candle.

There's a figure moving behind the window of the shed. Do I
put my hand over Agnes's mouth, or invent a story—a game—
as I pull her out of sleep, as we run into the trees?

But it's only Paul. With an axe. Moving toward the heap of unsplit wood.

When we came back—Agnes still wrapped with the yellow characters, thrilled by our adventure—he'd been asleep on the hard wood of the dock. He sat up, then stood, as we approached, and said nothing, and helped with the ropes, and then I let him hold me. The silence existed alongside Agnes, who was a flood of accounts—There was a guy buying a piece of a cow—and I felt the clench in his stomach, too, and Agnes was still going—And Mama peed on her shoe!
    Please, such a tiny bit.
    A lot.

The most terrifying thing that ever happened, on one of those nights in the woods, was my hand landed on something that wasn't a tree, it was smooth and soft, but hard, too, it was a face, and I was shot out of my body, and then I heard my brother's voice, and it was him, he'd followed me.

The cards are still scattered across the floor—the storm having blown through the house, its windows left open, along with everything else—and I sweep them into a pile, shape them into a neat, dirty stack. I line the rocks and bone and skin and mussel shells along the windowsill. I'll teach her, next, how to play war.

·

The airtime was reserved for something more drastic; no one's quite willing to say yet we got off easy. There's a segment about an eagle's nest that was blown out of its tree; a camera crew has been filming the family as they try to regroup; conservationists are on hand if they're needed. It's a pledge drive day. Maybe next time, I say, and turn it off. But thank you.

I never gave much thought to why my brother came looking for me, in the dark. I never imagined what it was like, to have been *found* in that way.

I wade through the waist-deep ferns and come out onto the little promontory that looks eastward toward the sound. To the south, the ocean is moving—a great roiling darkness like a shadow, headed this way. Where my heart was: a fish.

The roiling begins to break apart into fragments of black and fragments of white, into a dozen, then dozens, of distinct shapes.

Eiders.

On the wing.

Low, low, low.

Then out beyond the sound, gone.

At dusk, I take Agnes walking through the ferns, hoping to hear it, the *gronk*, for a chance to say *buttermunk*, and squeeze her hand, to see what she'll understand. What she'll take and what she won't.

•

But it *was* weird. As the folks on the radio were getting at. For a storm like that to come now. It wasn't that bad *here*, but it was bad. Down there. I'd nearly forgotten that part. I'm having a hard time keeping track of everything—what should cause dread, and what shouldn't. Maintaining the right perspective, always. Aside from everything, I know almost nothing about the arc of this place, the phenology, have only dropped down, occasionally. I've never seen things all the way through.

ONE THING AT A TIME.

I stick the letters on carefully.

The beach, too, is littered: Irish moss, shimmering purple clusters of tough flat fronds. The ocean is calm. I once saw my grandmother gather the stuff in her skirt—she wrapped it in cheesecloth and boiled it with milk and sugar. She gave us each a spoonful warm, then canned the rest.

I don't have milk or sugar or cheesecloth. But I have a stove, for now, and I have running water, and I have a reasonably clean sock I stretch until its porousness feels right to me. As it boils inside the sock, the weed releases its clear goo. I let it cool.

The jelly tastes like nothing, but feels good to eat, straight off the spoon.

Agnes knows what's funny better than I did at her age.

Take some to Papa.

Better her than me, I think.

We climb into the dinghy and I push us away from the dock, maneuver the oars into their locks. As we approach the ledge—beyond the shelter of the island, but visible—the seals slide off the rock to watch us from the water, before disappearing altogether. The family of ospreys doesn't budge from its nest at the top of the ledge-marking pole. They look shell-shocked, I think—three downy babies and a mother, huddled. Agnes and I clamber out of the boat, onto the uneven rock covered in slick weed—we hang on to it, in places, thick fist-fuls, to keep our footing. I lift Agnes to the high point then climb to meet her. I take from my pockets the yellow strip, torn from one of my grandmother's bedsheets, and tie the end of it, as tightly as I can, to the pole. Today, it hangs. Barely stirred by gentle breaths of wind.

We'll be able to see it, from the dock.

We'll be able to see what's really going on.

I know she was here, too. My mother. I know, when we were little, it must have been her, too, who gently held towels over our eyes when we leaned back, trustingly, in the empty tub, and she poured cup after cup of frigid water over the soap in our hair, as careful to keep it off the bare skin of our bodies as she was to keep it out of our eyes. I know that before these baths, she must have been with us in the cove. I know our father must have pinched her toes, too, as they flashed above the full stretch of sugar kelp, to get her kicking fast, back to the dock. I know she must have huddled us into towels, there in the warm sun, encasing us in protection against the things down there that wanted us for dinner. From our father, who sometimes failed to see when it was time to stop, who got so carried away.

I know she must have done these things. Any mother would.

You scare them.
    I do not.
    You get so wound up you don't think of anyone else.
    They're fine.
    You scare me.
    It could have gone like that.

Yes, I tell her, with confidence. You may eat the dandelions.

She has chewed and nearly swallowed the bitter yellow head before the taste catches up with her. Before she opens her mouth and puts out her tongue, covered with the bright mastication, like she doesn't know how to get it off.

Oh well, I say. Not so yummy.

A shiver racks her body.

Could we go ashore? Yes. But we stay.

She holds his hand like it's nothing. He holds her hand like he's held it all along.

We're going to the beach.

How lovely.

I watch them go down the path.

To distract myself, I walk to the far end of the island. Back to the duck blind, where I sit, and lose track of time, and name the oxeye daisies and the bayberry, until I panic, until I'm unable to close the distance fast enough, until the only name in my head is *Agnes*.

They're fine. They're curled up on the sofa, looking at pictures in the field guide I left on the cushion. Paul's making up facts about each marine mammal they encounter. Agnes, I see, is grateful. Or maybe she really believes him. Maybe she really believes pilot whales are born in clouds, that they don't take their first breath until they slam down into the sea.

Papa can make just about anything up, can't he, I say, mussing her hair the way I might his, if I were joking with him. It does not feel as good as I thought it might to have said this; the air has changed. Bye, he says, kissing the top of her head before he leaves the room, without looking at me.

I'm the shitty one? I want to scream.

I could go ashore to see Pettengill's response. Or I could stay.

DREDGE

I've been trying to imagine this place in March, when it's been empty all winter except for the spiders and the few little birds that have come down the chimney and starved or frozen in corners. When ice has dribbled its way out of cracks. I've tried imagining a very particular light hitting upon a very particular dust—skin maybe, but old, long forgotten, free to go. Dancing in the air.

The big news is: Paul's gone ashore to look for work.

If we're here, come March, will we be ghosts enough to see this emptiness? To be a part of it?

His skin looks better. He looked me in the eye when he said he was ready, when he said this was what had to be done. The smell of sick tiger that oozed from his pores is gone. Something for fast cash, he said, and I agreed—restaurant work, probably. Something just for now. He's so thin.

I'm not leaving him with Agnes.

We need the cash.

I don't want him having cash.

He was not the best server at La Cochina, the fanciest restaurant in our little Vermont town, but he was loved. He was allowed to bring home the unfinished bottles of wine left on tables, and he'd bring them straight to my house, and we'd

move from the dregs of one to the dregs of the next and he'd
explain to me why one cost $26 or $62 more than the other.
He would balance the empties on my stomach as I stretched
across the bed; if the bottle stayed standing, he lost.

What you are drinking, he said, is the essence of American
Resurrection. The grapes were coaxed into growing atop dusty
bluffs overhanging the Missouri River in a cicada year, and
it was initially feared the swarms would decimate the crop,
especially as the Mexican laborers had been able to send their
children to school that year without fear and there were fewer
hands on deck to stand sentry by the vines, prying off and
stomping the insects into the dirt; but the laborers soon saw
what was at stake and rightfully pulled their children, who
were given tennis rackets and baseball bats dredged from the
aisles of the Super Wal-Mart and told they could stop swinging
for a ten-minute break at noon, back to the fields. The corpses
of the bugs turned out to be fantastic fertilizer. Management's
only regret was that the cost of the sports equipment hadn't
been deducted from each worker's wages.

It's not funny, he said. Imagine if you didn't have this wine
to drink. I've said it before—thank god for management.

I couldn't quite bring myself to hand him the dead-man's key,
but I set it on the corner of the kitchen table. I told him it was
there. I did not watch him go.

I close every door and window and stand and look without
breathing. There are cobwebs sagging in the corners of the

windowpanes, a spider. The ball of cut glass, hanging from a piece of fishing line, sending tiny rainbows over the room. The table is sagging with decades of moisture, its surface spotted with mildew. There are no sounds.

But Agnes is sleeping on the other side of the wall, air moving in and out of her lungs, dreams running through her mysterious skull. This air might as well be her breath.

I let my own breath out. I open the windows.

The spider, I notice, is wrapping a moth.

I try, instead, to smell my mother.

I smell my own hair just in case.

It smells of woodsmoke, baked salt, Agnes.

LICK

We peel back the wrappers and begin. It slides down the length of our fingers, over the humps of our knuckles. It hits our wrists and we lick it off. Hers was a rocket pop. Mine a Häagen-Dazs—classic vanilla milk chocolate almond. Mostly melted from the journey over. But still.

How much do they pay? I ask. I'm married, now, to a man who drives an ice cream truck.

It's just for now.

You get tips?

These ants are out of their minds. I'm not sure they've ever had Red Dye 40.

I hand what's left on my stick to Agnes; I want her to have the protein. I don't actually think he answers, but maybe I missed it. There's so much going on.

You okay? I try my hand on his knee.

My brain is unfocused. I don't know what's more urgent: my need to pee or talk more or lie down. The heart needs to slow down, the heart needs to speed up. It's the sugar, partly. I go to lie down, leaving bright-mouthed Agnes with this ice cream truck guy, just for a minute.

•

In the dark, I sit up and look at his shape.
    People once thought that butterflies came from mud.
    People have said that man rose out of the dust.
    When morning comes, the colors begin at our toes.

DRIFT

HAMMER

I disregard the needling of the radio.

I return to the bed, and lie down, and am very still.

I've done this each night for three nights.

Paul goes ashore, and he returns, on schedule.

Everything is fine.

Agnes has the tiny wet shell between two fingers, so close to her lips she's almost kissing it. She'll get this. I'll teach her to whistle, then to swim.

Hi, Charon! There's her boat, moving across the sound, gathering up all the little winged things for their journey. She's too far to see me waving, of course.

That's it, I say to Agnes. Keep them moist. Like this.

His tinkling music must bring them running. I wonder how the mothers see him, when they do. I wonder what dogs bark at him. How long until his first paycheck. Why he chose me. What questions he'd answer, if I asked.

I can name every plant growing along this beach. I know which way the terns will turn, a millisecond before they do it. I know that at night the crabs will come up from the sand to feast on fleas—so many thousands of their indifferent glistening green bodies, an entire army from another place—from another planet, it seems, that it's better not to look. Better not to see the world so overturned, when it'll be back to normal in the morning.

FAITH

Agnes is watching the ants. We have a habit of separating insects into classifications of good and evil. Earthworms are good; the caterpillars that covered the porch and shingles of the house when we first arrived, that spewed their toxic hairs into the wind and made us itch in a relentless way, were, of course, evil. The ants, which have forged a path between the sliding door and the floor beneath Agnes's chair, some of them even beginning to venture up its legs and onto the table, pointing out my failure to have adequately wiped it down, represent neither category, exactly—instead introducing the concept of some loftier categorical terrain from which judgment and redemption flow. It was I who left the crumbs.

With my eyes on Agnes I can tell it's coming. She's intent on a single ant that's carrying half of another dead ant on its back. The question might come from any direction. Righteousness, if I'm lucky. More likely: Death. Grief.

Mama, she says, and I feel the flip of panic.

Mama! she says again.

Yes, baby?

Where Papa is?

How she reads my mind I'll never know.

It's eight o'clock already, on the solstice—the longest day of the year.

•

A breeze has come up and rustled things, set rainwater loose from the broad leaves of the oaks. There's something in the shape of his body—the blanket twisted around his legs?—that makes him look like a baby. He came in late, when I was asleep, but there's no other problem I can prove exists, no reason to worry.

I put a fingertip on his shoulder and wait for his eyes to open. Eventually, his eyelids flicker, and he watches the sunlight, too, until he falls asleep again, pulling air in loudly—the hangover of withdrawal like a cold that won't let up, a deep congestion—and I listen to rain that's not really rain, and watch the colors moving over the bed, deepening and fading as the branches of the firs move in the breeze, interfering with the light.

Agnes begins her morning calls.

Want a cup, Mamaaa, she's saying.

You do? I say, with mock surprise, when I arrive. And what do you want in your cup? Coffee?

Milk, she shouts.

Ah, I say.

How she's forgotten we don't have any, I can't know.

From myself I'm still guarding the fact that we don't have any coffee.

I have an idea, I say, at the bottom of the stairs. Let's go look for those hips.

But it's still too early; they're as green as Granny Smiths.

They make us pucker. Their tart seeds spread over our tongues, hairy.

•

What do you know about Blake? he says. I've left the book on the table.

I shrug. What's in there.

Good enough, he says.

Ashore, baby, I tell her again, midday. Ashore. Papa has gone ashore.

Maybe I, too, should just buy her a Popsicle, instead of keeping her alive.

WHISTLE

A rotten apple blew off one of the trees, hitting my head with mealy force.

There was a little juice in my hair, which had been whipped into strands by the wind. I rubbed at it with the hem of my dress. The bees were quick.

You know what it means, said Jess. She picked up the fallen apple and twisted it into two halves, revealing its double arcs of little black seeds.

We were on a friend's orchard, in Vermont—a few friends, Paul's friends really, to cheer us on. Our U-Haul was packed and ready for Pittsburgh, a city neither of us had ever seen. Paul had a job. I'd find something, too; it didn't matter. Whereas Paul had ideas for a career, was heading down a path, I was drawn to work that could be picked up and abandoned easily. For better or for worse, I found almost everything interesting. My education was solidly behind me.

Pregnant! said Vishan.

Guess I'm useless here, said Paul. His eyes were brighter than ever against the brown tweed suit he'd thrifted. All day, actually, he'd had a new energy about him that I pretended didn't make him feel far away.

All right, I said. Let's not be crass.

A bee entangled itself in my hair. Its panic was a rising pitch, a tiny, alarming vibration against my scalp. Then there were two—maybe more. Paul lifted strands of my hair, cupping one bee, and then another, scooping them away from my head. Everyone wants you today, he said, into my ear. And you're mine. It wasn't the bees anymore, it was pleasure. Buzzing there.

From wherever he was, he was choosing me.

An apple did it, we could say. We're having an apple child.

It was a story I could imagine my new husband telling her, our future child.

She was what—the size of a bean? Not quite a peach pit. Far from a banana.

The box contained three tests and I'd used them all, in part because I didn't trust the way I peed on them.

Open your eyes, I'd said.

His eyes did not light up. He did not grab my hand.

Like this, I said, showing him the tip of my pinkie.

You're sure?

A crow landed on an outer branch and the mass of starlings lifted into the air. When it settled back into the tree, the crow, up top, didn't make a stink. It flapped its heavy wings and headed off for someplace else. I wanted it back.

Of all the moments of my life, I wanted this one back.

Hadn't he said to me, You'll make an incredible mother? And then it became a thing I could imagine becoming?

•

Ashore. A shore. Ash ore. Azure. Assure.

The stranger it becomes, the more sure I am there's something in it.

I've decided to see things differently—to see that I'm not good. The belief that I'm good, it's dawned on me, has been destructive.

I consider how close to ruin I've led my family. By choosing blindness. The decision to view myself through a lens of badness, I think, will be good. Instructive. Eye-opening.

And it hits me: being a *sinner* is helpful to some.

Clarifying.

It gives you somewhere to go.

This hunger can be the space I occupy next, when it's ready. When the hole is whole. The pit round and pure. Everyone comes from somewhere. I'll give everything there is to Agnes. Only my eyes will eat.

Tucked into the corner of the bathroom mirror, on a piece of loose paper, in my grandmother's hand: *Let the words of my mouth, and the meditation of my heart, be alway acceptable in thy sight, O LORD, my strength and my redeemer.*

Thinking you're being watched: helpful?

•

She keeps telling me not to follow her. I try to keep a respectful distance. I pretend to look at everything but her. It's not like the dizziness that made me sit. It's a new feeling like I'm moving with the branches, the ferns, blowing. It's easy to move like this.

He doesn't always come home when he should, but he has reasons. There hasn't been money yet, aside from the scrap of tips, but there are reasons. It's been two weeks.

Down among the needles three yellow jackets are crawling over a bright red flower that's fallen from somewhere. I move closer and bend down and see it isn't a flower—it's the opened chest of a small bird, this brilliant inside red shocking and tender against the muted browns of the parts normally exposed to the world. The bees climb up and over one rib bone and then the next, up and over each other, with no clear goal.

When I stand, I have to fold back over, plant my hands on my knees.

At the high center of the island, I show Agnes how to make the seeds of the jewelweed pop off with the touch of a finger. I let her feast on the soft orange petals while I scan the sparkling bay.

But there's no yellow dory. There's no Charon. Just irrelevant boats, far away, moving about in a world that doesn't overlap with ours.

I feel the feeling that is like my brain is being used for fuel, and scan the field for things to eat. For Agnes.

I can't get over to check the kits, in this arrangement. Paul has the boat.

And yet I know. I know with peaceful certainty that none of it matters—that humans are doomed, our time is coming to an end, anyway.

I know well enough to enjoy this moment.

Soon this whole place will be swallowed up.

I can see it so clearly: The sugar kelp reaching the tops of the trees; a world underwater, weightless, a new beginning.

And what a relief it will be: this sure destruction. What lightness will come with it.

Her face will greet us on the watery porch, her floating dark hair a wild crown, the surprise on her face replaced with a welcoming smile. Instead of orange slickers there will be her aged body, a second crown below. We'll swim toward her and see that this has been her home, all along.

Paul is still gone. It's been a night and a day.

I sit with Agnes on the porch in a patch of sunlight and tickle the bottoms of her feet with the tip of a giant fern frond. She grabs it and rustles its soft stickiness under my chin.

Ticka, ticka, ticka, she says.

This morning, we watched a jellyfish with long, tangled tendrils billow beneath us as we stood on the gangplank. Chop it! Agnes yelled. The machete was in my hand. The strange, stretching thing was moving, but were we? No good, I said. Was I the jellyfish? We went out in the dinghy for more dulse, for her, until I got scared. Until I lost track of what was water and what was sky, and which way I needed to take us.

•

Lie down, I tell her. Here. Our bellies are full of seaweed. I wasn't ready to be reborn. The kitchen stinks. I rub my hand on the warm wood.

A good thing about us being stuck over here is that it means the dory is on the other side. Dad could climb into it as easily as Paul. Dad could show up at any time. As long as the boat is over there. As long as Agnes and I are stuck.

So could anybody.

The sun moves fast at this hour. I'll go get a blanket to put over her prickling, shaded flesh.

On the beach, one of her buoys, yellow and brown, the line snapped.

We're out drawing faces on little rocks, leaving them in secret places.

The ink skips over the tiny bumps. *We're here.*

It floats where it lands. The tide's on its way out.

The truck blew a tire, he says. His manager wouldn't pay him for the lost hours; he worked late, instead. It made more sense to sleep in the car. The dory doesn't have lights.

Two flies that followed him in are thwacking against the window screens. I watch him stand there, waiting, right next to the fly swatter hanging on a nail on the wall. He leaves the room like this is going to be impossible if I choose to never believe him. I haven't said a word.

After a minute I grab the swatter and smack the fucking flies myself.

Here, he says.
    I count it: $76.
    So you get paid on Fridays? I say.
    He hesitates.
    It's easy, I say. Fridays, or not?
    Yeah, he says. Fridays.
    What would an agonist do?
    Great, I say. So next time should be for one week, or two?
    How long would an agonist hold this smile?
    Two.

In the full sun of the beach, it's a perfect day: It's possible, of course, that I'm crazy. And wrong, and ungenerous. That everything is fine.

And she's got it! From between her lips is the wisp of a whistle, and I remind her to lick them, and then it's stronger, and steady. And there comes the little slug, from her bright yellow shell, to see what's calling her forth.

POUND

There are days of hard, pounding rain; days when I can't wake up on the heels of nights when I can't sleep. Staying in the house feels too much like staying inside my skull—I feel like someone in a room with a ten-second movie on loop. Agnes's grouchiness is part of that loop, and my inadequate way of handling it.

We go out into the rain.

The roots of the trees are slick and dark; the rain pummels us as we jump them, our bare feet squishing back into the shifting, liquid earth.

Don't step on a snake! Agnes yells, as my feet leave the ground.

Wouldn't think of it! I say, as I land.

I want to keep running, to tear through the woods clear across the island, to watch the rain batter the ocean. I hop neatly over a root.

Don't step on a snake! Agnes yells again.

A snake? I gasp, playing.

No—say *wouldn't think of it*, Mama!

And so. A three-second movie on repeat. In order to keep the peace. In order to be good.

I know she's plucked these snakes right from where she found them, nestled, but awake, from the cracks in me.

Does it matter if he comes? What use is he, until two weeks

from now? What good is my doubt until then? What harm is my hope? In two Fridays, I'll know.

Our lungs and hair and clothes hold the smoke. I've kept the stove going to fend the dampness off. Smoke leaks back into the room from the grates on the side of the heavy cast iron, and from the places on top it's rusted through—thinning, until it's just gone. Every few hours, I throw the windows open, letting all the damp back in, for fear that Agnes will suffocate.

At night, I wake and creep into her room, lift each of her windows up four inches as the rain thuds through the canopy and onto the roof and batters the earth outside, pulling dirt and a season's worth of fallen pine needles into new little rivers, leaving rock and root exposed.

I've got bowls out, all around the yard. To catch the rain. Without gas, the generator doesn't power the water pump. The kits could be selling, I remind myself.

Three days and he hasn't come home.

I bring the box to the kitchen and choose a red trip of vinyl. **FRAME THY FEARFUL SYMMETRY.**

This rain will be a fine excuse.

Even after I found her in the barn I knew there was something true in what I'd seen. The image of my mother floating in the creek.

By the time she started leaving a bedroll out there, not even in the loft but right outside the doors of the pens, where the horses slept, standing, her life among us was a delicate thing my brother and father and I protected by saying nothing. We knew any word might be the last stone—the one to send the birds up and away for good, landing beyond our sight.

So? I said, when Conrad told me. When the horses were gone, it was clear she was, too. So? A pebble, dribbling out of my mouth.

The bees, I've learned, from books upon my grandmother's shelves, were not in fact bees. They were yellow jackets, which are wasps, and they were not drinking the blood of the little exposed bird like so much sweet nectar, as I'd imagined. Adult yellow jackets don't eat meat—they wouldn't think of it. But what they will do is hunt and scavenge for flesh and make it into a kind of syrup to give to their babies, if it's needed. If there's a nutrition emergency.

I suppose it's some relief to not be daughter and mother all at once.

The rain has stopped. The night is ghostly.

Someone left bolts on top of the cardboard box, and ocher rings, left by the rust, bleed out like eclipses. I found the box in the shed. Inside are three two-minute hand flares and a package of fluorescent water dye. It looks like there used to be a distress whistle as well, but it's gone.

Agnes has been asleep for hours. I was asleep, too, next to her, until I woke up.

I've always known that using a flashlight is dangerous: Anything will see you before you see it. But this is an island.

We're alone. Inside my beam, the molecules stir in a slow frenzy. I make my way. I cast my beam over the water, but it quickly gets lost in the frenzy. It can be impossible, finding your way back to this place in the fog. I should have put a light out, a beacon.

But the dory's right there.

Tied to the side of the dock.

I light up his body, on the boards. His head's on top of a life vest. His arms are pulled into his sodden jacket, the sleeves empty. He's breathing.

I should check his arms. His pockets, at least. I could know things. The price is he might wake up.

By his feet is a five-gallon jug of diesel. I pick it up. It's half-full. It bangs against my leg as I carry it up the hill.

Tuck, he says.

He's in the kitchen now, in the horrible morning light, and looks awful, standing there, the ghostliness not gone from him, only from these wretchedly bright surroundings, his arms at his sides, bowed and uncertain.

It was the rain. I couldn't.

If I keep my back to him, give him berth, maybe he'll just disappear.

It worked with my mother, in time.

I wake up and the fire's out. It's been nine weeks since my grandmother died. Twelve weeks until we'll have to go. Nothing but smoldering gray ash on the stones in front of my face.

It's true: I'd like for him to keep the fire going. It's a thing he would have done, before.

I find his pants. I take the boat key from his pocket. Maybe he does still have a job. More likely he doesn't.

We've got the kits. We've got nearly ninety days. We've got my dad out there, somewhere.

A gull has its wing tipped toward the water.

The gull's cousin, the albatross, sets the record. Ten thousand fucking miles, without landing.

The faith in me wants to settle.

BUSINESS

REPLY

My suspicions about this woman's motivations persist. Some things couched inside some other things. Pity inside compassion? And something greedier. A new sticker on her car says: LOVE YOUR BEAN GROWER.

She pulls me and Agnes into a hug.

Her drapey blouse is unbelievably soft.

Agnes, released, stiffens. She has seen the puppet rack. Mozart and Curie and more RBGs and—oh my god, what the fuck, those ears, the stitching on the face, that one should not have made it into production.

Look at her! You like this one? She's reaching for the president-monkey. You must have been born under Obama, just barely. Thank heavens, right? she says to me.

All set, I say.

Of course she wants one—he's her president! Want me to just take it out of your check?

I endure until that check, for the full $21.25, is in my hand.

Outside, the question I know is coming: Where's Rumpelstiltskin?

I'm not sure, baby.

I last saw Rumpelstiltskin napping in the wrack while we placed the stones about, and suspect he's gone with the tide.

I roll the windows down to let the screams out. I roll them up in the hope people will stop looking at me this way.

WELCOME, IMMIGRANTS!
HUG A BLACK BOY TODAY
OFF WITH HIS HEAD
I SURVIVED OBAMA SO SUCK IT
Money in my pocket.
Which doesn't quite distract from the fact that we're going to the library. To see what's come from Pettengill.

My fiduciary duty is to enact the expressed written will of your grandmother, which, as regards the island property, was clear and without caveat: It is to go to your father, as long as he is living. As you may know, your grandmother left what other assets she had to the Marine Conservation and Research Society, and to the Friends of Saint Luke's; in other circumstances, such assets, were they left in a trust for this purpose, might be used by myself, as an exercise of my obligations, to keep current all amounts owed on the property in question— namely, annual property taxes, mooring fees, and critical maintenance costs. In actual circumstance, if your father is not located, and not proven to be deceased, my obligation will be to protect for him the closest financial equivalent of the inherited property, until such time as he decides to collect it.

Still nothing from my father. Who is not located. Who is not proven to be deceased.

At the end of the row of computers, a toddler is throwing a fit, demanding that his mother acknowledge that he is not a pretzel person. The inside of his mouth, I can see, is full of unresolved pretzel matter. We lock eyes and for a second he stops, then shrieks louder. Agnes is staring at him, too.

My obligation will be to protect for him the closest financial equivalent of the inherited property. The fog around my brain is thick. *My obligation equivalent. My inherited obligation. My financial property.* There's a space in my chest where my heart used to be. My body understands something. I read it again.

There's a man with a weird look on his face grinning at Agnes. He's scooting his chair closer. He's poking her in the ribs.

We're up, out, gone.

BET

I keep coming back to the idea that she maybe thought this island would bring him back. For us. That she didn't intend to leave me with nothing. That she believed her dead hand could guide him back.

I wonder if all faith is reckless. What tips the scale to make it useful. How important it is to put a fine point on what, exactly, you're giving yourself over to, what you're gambling on, or with—to put it down in so many words. I wonder what ridiculous thing I'd be faced with, if I did it. What words would watch me from the page, or from the corner of the mirror. If unexamined faith is more, or less, ridiculous than that which has been studied, prodded, made explicit.

I wonder if, in the end, there is any faith other than that which is necessary. And so, forgivable.

RECEIVER

I come down out of the trees. The boat is gone.

Paul!

Papa!

The trick, with Agnes, is to make it feel like a game.

We run along the paths again, and then through the house. Paul! Papa! But of course I know. I lift the coil of rope behind the shed, and the dead-man's key is gone.

Who would have thought that my plan wouldn't work? Who would have thought that on eleven acres, I could have kept hidden from a drug addict a thing the size of a dead minnow?

Ashore? Agnes says.

I nod. I smile.

Ass whore.

It's not that I'd made zero effort to get help. To not be an idiot. From the pay phone across from the library, after I'd stopped hiding in the duck blind and come ashore and looked up the stuff in the packets that had just upended and clarified my world, I called the only pay-what-you-can detox center I could find. They couldn't take him, they said. People were dying, daily. Heroin, fentanyl. He wouldn't die from this, they said. In any case, he'd have to call himself. You can't sign someone else up for detox.

I'd had to make a split-second decision: *kray-tum*, or *kra-tm*. The difference between *aunt* and *aunt*. High or low. I went high, *krah-tm*, which was just one more reason to dislike myself.

He's going to lose everything, I said. I just wanted them to know.

You're sure it's only kratom he's using?

He doesn't care if his daughter has food.

We just—haven't seen kratom as a problem. We have twelve beds, that's it.

Is there somewhere else I can try?

If you can pay. Sometimes insurance will help. I wish I had different answers. You're sure it's only kratom?

Hundreds of dollars of it a day.

Was I proud now that my husband was so special? The only one in the entire universe to have this problem?

He's not *alive*. We're—

But there I was, in front of Agnes, in front of all the people walking across the square. I put the receiver down.

We were what? I'd been given so many advantages in life. So many advantages I just didn't know what to do with.

Nightfall, and he's still not home. And Agnes won't sleep: The sky is exploding. By the time I cave and let Agnes into my own bed, her voice is hoarse from calling.

Why the sky booms, Mama?

It's fireworks, baby.

Why you didn't come?

I stroke her sweaty forehead. Want to see?

We walk through the dark woods, with only the strange, periodic light—purple and blue and red—scattering to the south. The delayed crack and boom. We sit down on the dock, Agnes on my lap. If she notices that the boat is still gone, she doesn't say.

In addition to the main show over the city, people along the coast, and some on the other islands, are sending their own fireworks up.

I lean back and press my palms against the cool wood, let Agnes's head settle against my chest. I'd always liked this feeling, watching the show at Derby time with thousands of others lined up with chairs and blankets and bags of Doritos along the Ohio. How the explosions had quieted us all as we felt them inside our bodies, how each of us probably kept quiet in order to listen and feel for some message, for something that was meant just for us. How when we didn't understand it, we licked bright powder off our fingers and sucked at Mountain Dew.

My last year of high school, the year Dad left, too, and I stayed in the house with Conrad, I hopped trains with a guy I met at the Chinese restaurant where I took to-go orders over the phone, and he washed dishes. He was there the night one of our regulars called in.

You'd like what? I said, thinking I'd misheard him.

Szechuan the counter, he said again.

Set you on the counter. He wants to have sex with you, my dishwasher boyfriend-to-be explained to me.

We were stalled in a yard outside Muskogee when the fireworks began. We were sitting on the little porch of a grain hopper. The train finally started rolling, and as the night darkened we saw the lights going off over fields and across rivers and, as we passed through towns, right above our heads. Bottle rockets screamed and exploded against the metal sides of the cars next to ours; we pulled our legs into the little vestibules of space.

I like fireworks, Agnes says. Fiyawooks. She's in my lap still, both of us reclining, the back of her head still resting against my sternum, the vibrations moving through both of us. The water reflects the chemical colors in the sky. At each explosion, her head presses harder into my bone.

I like seeing what everyone else is seeing, I say.

I wonder what, of this, makes sense to her. What message she's receiving.

When the fireworks stop—when it's just the stray popping off over one island or another, or over the mainland—we go to sleep, together, in her bed. In the morning, we catch two small crabs and fill a bucket with bladder wrack. A fish has washed up but it stinks. Its eyes are already gone.

The motor makes its usual low gurgle. I wish Agnes were asleep so I could leave her, so I could go and rip his throat out. I stand at the top of the gangplank, looking down at him as he climbs out of the boat. Agnes stands next to me. He looks up and gives me a wave.

What are you doing? I say.

He cocks his head, looks at me.

Got some groceries, he says. With one finger he holds up

the plastic bag he's carrying. I can see the hard edges of boxes. Crackers and spaghetti, I'm guessing.

I shake my head.

Fuck you, I say.

He nods once, comes clomping up the ramp. Drops the bag at my feet as he squeezes past me and continues up the path. Agnes follows after him.

I was right: crackers and spaghetti. Plus: six eggs in bright white Styrofoam, a slim box containing strawberry Pocky.

Fuck you. Fuck you, fuck you, fuck you.

I stare hard at the oak that bends out over the water. It does not split. It does not fall crashing.

I need the key, I say. He's on the floor with Agnes, pushing acorns around.

I'm not staying here. It's ridiculous.

I just need the key. Right now. I need to go over.

He looks at me.

Just give me the key, I need to go over. I'm bleeding all over myself, okay.

We both know that I've won for the moment.

There's not much gas. I was going to get some tomorrow.

I wait until the key is in my hand.

Of course you were.

I take Agnes, who doesn't want to come, and we do go out in the boat, but not ashore. When we're past the ledge, I cut the motor. The yellow strip is hanging limp. She watches me heave and pats me on the knee as we drift.

I haven't had a period since she was born.

I wonder if there's enough gas to get back to the island, then ashore again tomorrow. I let the anchor over.

Smile, Mama? she says.

And I do. Because I have the key.

Because I understand absolutely everything, and know what I have to do.

At the bottom of the path, behind the dead pine tree with the lichen creeping up its side, along the bare branches, I dig a hole with my fingers and drop it in. I cover it back up with soil and pine needles, and move a stick over it. Growing a boat, Mama? Shh, I tell her. A secret. On the walk back up, I make sure he's nowhere he might have seen.

There's nothing to be gained from talking about it. I just won't let him have it.

It's not an argument he wants to have directly, either.

All night long I cannot stop the shaking. I gather more and more blankets—there must be thirteen, fourteen of them, around me. I wonder if one or two more will do the trick.

MY FATHER

Agnes and I make the rounds, collecting our money. I'm no longer in danger of cracking at the smallest show of kindness from these people who pay me. Give me my money, I think, as I smile.

We go to the library.

We go to the supermarket.

We do it all again.

Anyone who has more than they need can get on down to hell. Including those who have $9.95 to spend on a bumper sticker kit and some dire message to share with the world. Including those whose carts are full with this and that bullshit, and are watching me as Agnes screams because I won't let her have one of the slow-moving lobsters in the tank, yellow bands disarming their claws, which they've given up on even trying to use.

NEWS

What we were not expecting today, in the least, holy shit, was this email from my father. But what lead-up is there to an email—what turn in the air, what change in behavior of the birds? None. No techno sky to scan for an incoming. Not even the crunching of gravel under the mail carrier's feet. No barking of dogs.

Not there, then there. From nowhere.

The jail itself was not so bad but they can do anything they want to you. Keep you starve you. There was one guy they kept telling him his wife was with his enemy now and he kept two versions of her alive in his head one he loved and one he despised.

I wonder who else can hear my heart; if they can see it pounding. They must.

He'll tell me more, the words on the screen say, but for now, he's figuring out what to do next. For now, he's in Belize. For now, he's at an internet café, and wants to make his way home. *I thought I preferred this direct brutality free of the Psychological Warfare of the States but now I have really seen what human life is worth down here.*

These words do not say anything about any of the dozens of emails he may or may not have read. From me, from the executor.

Agnes is playing with the wires beneath my station—*fine*, I think. I think of immovable granite. I think of sharp, cutting slate under my bare feet. I think of the pull of my fingernails away from my flesh as I attempt to pry open a clam. Of a barnacle slicing my knuckle. I open my eyes.

He is not *proven to be deceased.*

I try to keep it simple. I try to not overwhelm him.

When you say home, I write, *where do you mean?*

I follow a Reddit thread about back doors in dealer sites—internet doors you can pass through only once you've spent enough money in the public-facing market, new rooms where the names of the products change, and prices are higher.

> *Shit their so dollar but if u got it its potant*
>   *My bruh tried that shit and got drained stay away*
>   *Ur bro sounds weak man*
>   *Yep EX-MARINE real weak good luck*

The handle I create is Tuckedinforthenight. Because one world isn't enough to navigate.

Has anyone out there bought from Speciosa Supply? Had problems?

For the ten minutes we have left, we wait and watch.

CHANGE

I lament and lament and lament the loss of his mind until it hits me: It's me that's changed. Not his mind. His mind was always bent this way; it's what made him feel so right to me, a sympathetic force against a strange and looming world.

Mom was right. We loved him more. I did, anyway; Conrad may have chosen to go with her, if he'd been given the option. If she hadn't told him to go back to sleep.

I wonder if she hadn't made up her mind until she said those words. If she'd been watching him, on the fence, until the moment he woke, and looked at her. I wonder if it was instinct or decision. *Go back to sleep.*

I know I'm not supposed to say *crazy*. Regarding Dad. Regarding anyone. He lives by truths unapparent to others. He looks off the rails because we cannot see his rails. I used to see them; they were mine; they ran right through my house.

TABULATE

The disappointment is hard to take, day after day. A week gone
by, and nothing in bold in my in-box. Nothing new. Nothing
life-changing. I can't tolerate the stillness.

I heard from him, I write to the executor. *He said he's coming. Did you hear from him?*

And then, later, the tick of worry: This is how I'll lose this
place. By giving it away.

On Reddit: nothing.

What if I put it on paper? What if I wrote: *Though I have been
given but little sign, I believe in your return, your salvation, the
power of your love.* What if that looked back at me from the
mirror every morning?

WHEN IS FAITH EXCUSABLE?

EXCHANGE

In my dreams, when he comes up the path, he goes to the tool-shed first. And he's in there too long. The time I have to wait for him to come out and do what he is going to do is long enough to wake me up. The Executor.

Paul's withdrawal, this time, is shorter. Until the fourth day, I can feel his anger through the walls, the blame for all this pain. On the fifth day he can be found, weeping, on the couch.

I had no intention of ever being righteous about a single thing in my life. I had no intention of ever being any of this.

What now?

RESOURCE

I twist off the end of the flare. The fog is heavy and low; I can't see thirty feet beyond the dock. I strike the end of it. It sputters a few bright orange embers into the water, then goes out. The smell is like battery acid.

So now I know.

What I have left are two of these flares, that will sputter brightly, for a second and a half.

OFFER

Out there, past the ledge, is the boat with the face. Come, I say to Agnes, and we go, up to the house, into the kitchen, where I take the box from atop the fridge. Ignoring Paul, who is sitting there, staring at a book I can't see the title of. Who glances at me questioningly—wondering, I think, if I've forgiven him. I look down at the fiery eclipses.

Back on the dock, I twist and strike. Nothing. I do it again, with the third flare. The last of its kind. It gives off a good two seconds of falling chemical flame as I hold it, half-heartedly, above my head. I turn my body away from the wind, to get the stuff out of my face. Across the distance, I see her arms waving over her head. I can't quite commit, but give a little wave back, like I'm saying hello.

As she approaches, I can see she hasn't taken care of her skin. She might be forty. She might be fifty. She might be sixty. She's strong, her body a tool. I can feel her making her own assessment as she sidles the boat against the dock—but whatever idea she's come up with, it's nothing crucial. Nothing hangs on it. I do not determine her fate. My jeans are loose. Our hair tangled. There is still a faint handprint in the blue wool of Agnes's sweater. What this woman can't see is that Agnes's name is written in full, in Sharpie, on the flesh between one of her tiny shoulder blades and the other. As the boat makes contact, the gull perched on the stack of empty traps in the stern flies

up, circles, and lands in the same spot, its single leg stretching
back down to grab at the wire. Agnes is leaning into me; my
fingers are rubbing the soft lobe of her ear. The bright blue
barrels are full of dead fish with big open eyes.

Everything good? she says. Her eyes, which had gone to
Agnes, are back on me.

I can tell from her voice that she's shouted over plenty of
wind.

But she's alone. I've only ever seen her alone.

There's wet light glinting off the mottled shells shifting inside the big white tub behind her.

Agnes twists her head, and I realize how hard I'm squeez-
ing her lobe. I let it go. The fish is in my chest.

Just testing, I say. Didn't think they'd work. My apologies.
We're fine.

I pull Agnes back in front of me and attempt to run my fingers through her hair. Now or never. The fish flops even more
wildly. I twist the untamed strands into a little bun, revealing
the sweet little hollow at the back of her neck.

I've got someone who can help you pull your traps.

I look away, allowing her to make of me what she will. It
was foolish—thinking this could possibly come off as an offer.
Rather than what it is. I take a breath to loosen my jaw.

My husband.

He's done it before?

Not exactly.

He can lift?

Yes.

Get up early?

Yes.

Listen?

Yes.

Stand the stink?

Yes.

For ten hours?

Painted, on the back of her boat: Rodney-Duane. The paint looks fresh.

She'll be back in the morning.

My thumb strokes the back of Agnes's neck, fits itself in to the nook. God's thumbprint, my grandmother said. The most she ever said about it. About God. Her finger resting there, in mine.

What we are left with for now are the three lobsters I've bought off her. Because sometimes a display is as valuable as anything.

EYES

GOD OF KNOWLEDGE

I think about the horses.

I never felt enough for them.

Could never muster the right sympathy.

Their too-big bodies seem to have evolved in a rush, without real thought.

They're a mess without us.

It just seemed sometimes like the right thing was to stop fixing them, give them a chance to evolve to fix themselves.

It was another case of colic, another horse rolling on its back that we were meant to diagnose more specifically. My classmates asked the right questions: What did the horse eat? When did symptoms begin? Could it get up? But I was stuck somewhere else: Why in god's name can't they vomit? How could we be expected to save these things, one after another, when they couldn't even do this basic thing for themselves?

I bring the water to boil on the woodstove, pausing to read a snippet off the page I tore from one of the *Gulf Conservationists* to crumple and light. Lobsters are biologically immortal. Their cells don't age. What does happen is their shells get damaged, introducing rot. Or they get devoured.

I leave the room when the high-pitched shriek begins. In

the scullery, I slide open the drawer where my grandmother kept the silver tools.

The drawer is empty. I pull open the other drawers, the cabinets, to look for them, to see what else is gone. Wasn't there once a crystal vase? A hand-thrown pitcher? A set of wrought-iron candelabras? When I turn off the heat, the three boiled bodies are bright, and still.

I tell Paul three things:

You will bring home all the cash you earn.

You will not set foot on the mainland.

You will not fuck this up.

I wonder how much he's trying to see the woman he married; how much he's making sense of someone new.

He waits at the dock before sunrise. She comes.

He waits at the dock before sunrise again, and she comes.

Even the weakest man, I guess, can thread a needle through all those open eyes. Even that must be of some use to her. Her knuckles, I saw, are like marbles. He does the banding, too.

Her name, I should mention, is Sharon.

What? he'd said, when he told me and I stared at him.

But what did I suspect him of, exactly? Possessing a secret portal into my brain, through which he ferried out bits he could use? To rattle my sense of the real? So he could use drugs unnoticed, my confidence gone?

He would unwind me for this, bit by bit, using his gift of knowing me. He'd create a schism. He'd make me jump my rails. His weakness an illusion. His knowledge his power.

•

I was jumping them then, considering it. My rails.

Things were good. Things were fine. Paul was clean and things were getting better.

Her name was Sharon, and Paul had nothing to do with it.

CATCH

HONK IF YOU'RE MY PAST CATCHING UP WITH ME.

White letters on green vinyl. Around the corner, gone.

Had I already collected for this one, or did it mean new money waiting?

I stack quarters, dimes, nickels, and pennies on the dash—four little grimy smokestacks—on a bed of bills: three ones, two fives, and a ten. A pleasing sequence.

Of course, there is only the present, which you have to navigate instant after instant after instant.

The bumper stickers may get us a little food. The lobsters will get us off the island.

Sharon pays cash, daily. An amount commensurate with their haul. He brings home, too, a few unfortunates: scrawny guys, but big enough to keep, that have lost a leg or two.

What does he think about, as he pushes the needle through eye after eye?

If Sharon knows the truth about him, will she cast him from her boat? What is he like out there?

What I can see, from my own places, is that there's no

further word from my father. That the cost of apartments is not going down.

What I can see is that someone has replied to Tuckedinforthenight.

Will try, thanks.

OPEN

In the hours before the sun is up, when he's still just a dark lump at the far edge of the bed, I lie awake. The bicycle he'd fixed up for me had gone missing in Pittsburgh. When the sun begins to rise, and he's gone, I sleep until Agnes wakes up. We eat bananas. We head to shore to check our kits. To visit the library to see what news, or lack of it, awaits us there.

He comes home in the late afternoon, aching and stinking. Worn back to what I'm used to. But bearing what he's earned.

The last letter I opened from her—the one that described her disorientation here—had been opened. *You're a dear girl and I imagine this could be useful to you.*

Maybe she hadn't just meant her descriptions. Maybe there'd been a check in there.

I make him give me the cash, before he even gets out of his skins. Before he hangs them on the peg outside the kitchen door. About $120, every day.

At this rate, we might have a home.

When October falls, we might be able to get off of here.

Have a lobster now, Mama?

When Papa comes home.

I spread the checkered tablecloth. By each of our plates is a rock, for the cracking.

I wonder if Agnes thinks that this is normal. If she even notices that we speak only through her.

I wonder if your papa likes catching lobsters, I say. Then, Like this, Apple. I show her how my grandmother's hands twisted the body into two separate parts: carapace with head, and tail. Yes, I can feel him watching not my hands but my face. Yes, I call her Apple, I think. And this version of her is only mine.

I wonder if Papa likes catching lobsters, I say to Agnes.

Tuck.

Do you think he can pull this off?

She wants to know what's what. What the frilly stuff, what the brown stuff, what the green stuff. What the heart? What the brain?

I don't know, I don't know, I don't know. And don't want to know.

Her hands—our hands—are shimmering and flecked with meat.

It's an open system, I remember—all of it, everywhere. Indistinguishable.

Agnes, I say. Papa is asking if we're okay.

You, he says. I'm asking you.

Do they communicate with words out there? With glances? Gestures?

•

I decide, for a day, to pretend that nothing has happened.

To imagine our lives are just beginning.

It's surprisingly easy. My anger drops away. I don't search for inconsistencies. I don't doubt the amount of cash he puts in my hand at the end of the day, wondering if I can confirm the amount with Sharon, without letting on. We eat our lobsters and the taste of the sea dribbles down our chins, and I ask him what he wants to do next. Like the world is his oyster.

He's hesitant, but says he's been thinking about massage school.

So this is what he thinks about. When he's staring at fish eyes. Not about how incredibly fucking sorry he is.

You want to touch people, I say.

Agnes is too busy dissecting to interrupt the silence.

I wonder how long it will last. That smell on your hands.

I suck the meat from a little leg.

What I'm really mad about is that the sight of him has broken my reverie, my progress.

I slide beneath the heavy covers, keeping as far as I can, as always, to my own side.

It feels fine, for now, being in the wrong.

Wanting his affection back.

Wanting him to *like* me, as he must like Sharon. To receive the new version of himself.

With the other body in me now—mine was a female, large but single-clawed—it feels more normal to be so many things at once. Less like being torn apart.

•

One of these days, I'll have a bath ready. I'll lift the washcloth to the base of his neck and squeeze. It will be my way of saying, I'm going to try now, too.

I worry about how to shield him from everything he's already done; I worry the past is insurmountable. I worry that my forgiveness can exist only so long as he refuses it.

I wonder, if I touch him, if he'll seem like less of a shadow. I worry, if I touch him, he'll become real again.

As real as he is on the boat. With Sharon.

Who keeps four pristine blue life vests strapped beneath the seat, near the fire extinguisher. Whose boot heel has been gnawed at. Who could surely afford a new set of boots, but sticks with this one. Who occasionally arrives with her Walkman still on her hip, and has only once left it playing when she slid the headphones down around her neck. The Stones. "Jumpin' Jack Flash." For the second before her thumb hit stop.

He could tell her all kinds of things about the Stones. If she would want to know.

In Pittsburgh, the car was towed from wherever he'd left it, and he needed me to go get it. I took a taxi to a faraway lot, all dirt and metal, where six dogs barked at me and infant Agnes while we looked behind heaps of scrap metal for a human to take the last of my money in exchange for our car.

I want him, what, to acknowledge every tiny piece of it? To say sorry, individually, for everything?

To take no pleasure in life until he's done it?

From the beach, I can see them coming. Agnes and I are in the water. My hands are latched beneath her belly. Kick, I'm yelling.

I've been trying out different Rodney-Duanes. A lover. A son. A father. A dog. A macaw she inherited from a neighbor. An ex-husband she's distilled into something of value.

I've been trying to imagine her standing on a floor. Lying in a bed. Standing before a refrigerator choosing what to eat before slumping onto a sofa, in front of a TV. As a regular human, on dry land.

I've never even seen her set foot on the dock.

My mother was in the kitchen. It was still an ugly day outside, full of wreckage from the heavy rain, and I was out of things to do. I stood in the doorway, watching her. My heart beat faster than was familiar, and a rushing rose up in my ears. She looked at me.

Will you braid my hair? I said. She'd finished with the horses.

Tuck, no, she said. *Why?*

The rushing sound pushed everything else out. I don't know if I stayed in the room or left. It didn't matter. I was inside my body; there was nothing but my blood and my pumping organs and a heat pushing out against my flesh.

You can ask someone into your world. But the price of refusal is steep.

•

Agnes, I say, my hands wet from her bath, my back to Paul, who's in the doorway. Your papa is asking if we can see he's doing better.

At the moment, the cash is behind the row of tallest books: $1,140.

You, he says quietly. I'm asking you.

RELEASE

I did go to the Department of Health and Human Services. They said I did not qualify for food assistance on account of the car. On account of owning a car.

It's worth $1,400, I said.

Yes, the woman agreed.

She was confirming what I already knew. That I was not entitled to help. That I should be able to fix this, myself. She was just helping me see myself, and my situation.

It was more beautiful than what you'd expect from a government agency, actually. They don't accept you until you're on your knees—until you have no chance of lifting yourself back up. I'd worried about the lines, and Agnes getting bored. I'd thought it would be a waste of a day.

I was not expecting to be given the choice: Fall, and accept the grace that comes with it, or don't.

I wasn't expecting the demands of a god. The offers that come with succumbing.

Back in the boat, it was something different: a great, floating detachment. A feeling of neither here nor there. A bit of a reverie.

Agnes, waving to the shoreline as we moved away from it, said, Bye, Earth.

What is the place she ferries him to? Where he comes back into himself? Where they talk like normal people? What would you call it? The place with no past, where he comes alive.

The bottom of our boat skips over little waves. *Thump, thump, thump, thump,* until the calm.

SKIN

SLOUGH

Having confirmed his existence—having fulfilled his own vague imperative to be alive to us, to maintain a foothold in our thoughts—my father, I must admit to myself, has dropped back off the face of the earth. It's only been ten days since his email, but I can tell he's gone. Maybe there is something, in the wake of an email. There are three new messages from the executor. I, too, have dropped off the face of the earth.

Silence, I think, is my only current asset. Silence, while I do some research of my own. While I see how bad my gaffe. How terrible my foolish urge to share the news with him—this man who may destroy me, at any moment, just by showing up. This stranger who is the only other person also waiting for my father. This stranger who, if only out of fiduciary obligation, wants to do him right.

I google: *maine probate statutes missing persons*. I read each statute three times, and begin to translate them sentence by sentence into regular language, the way I understand the lines of words, or think I understand them, on the pieces of scrap paper left out by the staff. I write with a dull two-inch golf pencil. I get through two and a half statutes before Agnes's boredom makes the task impossible. The words are a mess anyway. On the scraps. In my sodden sponge of a brain. I staple my scraps together using the chained-down stapler by the copy machine, and slip them into my pocket.

•

But I've caught a glimpse of something. I've seen that a lot might be tied up in this word, *missing*. That I can apply for receivership if I can prove him to be so. If he's been missing for five years.

Missing, though—how undelineated. I think of those Inuit with their fifty words for snow. How have we not, by now, developed a more precise language for human disappearance? *Can't* he be missing, and also heard from only ten days ago? Aren't those two things not necessarily contradictions? Isn't there room for us to burrow into the word, on our hands and knees, making the right tunnels that end, each one of them, at nothing?

Absconded
Lost
Disappeared
Escaped
Mislaid

That's all. And besides, the statute just says missing.

The statutes, themselves—my interpretations—are missing. Slipped from my back pocket. Gone.

I'm holding my shirt hem, making a little hammock for the beach things Agnes is depositing there: chiefly, today, bright orange crab shells, minus any legs, only slightly larger than quarters. My whole life, I thought these shells contained the dead. Only today have I learned they've merely been abandoned. The animals are out there. Their bodies slipped away. Vulnerable. Awaiting their new armor. Or already re-armored. Or dead.

We climb the big rocks and snatch up new goose tongue from the cracks, start a new collection in the hammock of my shirt. Scurvy grass. Sow thistle. We carry our salad-in-the-making to the soft clifftop with a view of ocean colliding with bay, where two days ago we saw that the sheet of low foliage dangled tiny white berries, a few of them showing the palest pink beginning to spread from beneath the leaves.

But the strawberries are gone.

The jagged rocks below are covered in gull shit speckled with seeds.

Irretrievable.

A crow calls from a treetop, a breeze carries the smell of the beach, a shadow crosses Agnes's face as we tromp down the path. Is this how the feeling gets in? The feeling that there's someone seeing us.

I stand straighter. I hold my shirt-basket proudly, casually, and ask Agnes what she's most excited to try. The goose tongue?

Cow, she says.

But I won't be deterred. I smile graciously.

She's out on the water with Paul, I know. But still. Some things about the world are inexplicable. Some feelings.

•

Also gone: my Reddit question. Just can't find it anywhere. I thought the internet kept everything.

The Germans must have them, I think. Words that are up to the task. I type *missing* into the translator tool and get:

Fehlt
Vermisst
Fehlend
Verschwunden
Verschollen
Verloren
Verirrt
Untergegangen
Verpasst
Irre gegangen

Maybe it's better to just have some foreign sounds. A set of unfamiliar syallables that mean what you need them to.

Aussichtslos
Ausgestorben.

Verpasst feels right. I let it run through my head. Each time, it's like the thing has already happened: The grief dredged from beneath the muck is already being carried away on the back of the tide.
Verpasst.

•

This I've learned: I can petition the court for receivership of the property, if my father is missing. If his missingness is, in fact, legal in nature.

Meanwhile, the state wants to see the land vest quickly, with somebody. The executor, on the other hand, has his own obligation to see it—or some financial equivalent of it—vest with my father. It's the job he was paid to carry out.

I decide to go check again. Who knows. How nice it would be for Agnes to know the taste of a strawberry!

We hold hands all the way down the center path. Even better, I take those hands and swing her in circles through the air. I laugh and lurch through the feeling that I'm going to go down, that the fragments at the edge of my vision are going to bleed in and consume it all.

Catch me!

Stop!

I grab her arm.

Up ahead: a red haze, hanging low over the grass. Where the ground dips just before it rises. A chemical fog, gathered there. Cupped, like so much poison. A spill from the plant up the coast. Something dropped by helicopters. When did we hear them last? Did I sleep last night? I put my hand over Agnes's mouth and nose, and stare, waiting for my vision to clear.

Sheep sorrel. Delicate red buds climbing the edges of grassy stalks. A haze of good fortune, of lunch. The delightful tang of rhubarb.

•

I wonder to what extent his body resists—tries to shake its way out of the labor. Under sun. In rain. I wonder what good the ropes do—if holding them is any help.

What has he told her of us?

Other words the online German dictionary suggests I see also, while I fuck around, in lieu of doing anything useful, in lieu of knowing how to make money appear more quickly: *irrer* (for madman); *kummerspeck* (for body fat gained in the face of grief).

Not a single kit has sold.

Agnes screams through the wall.

Need you, Mama. Want you, Mama.

I'm scared, Mama!

Why you not coming, Mama?

She goes at it so long her voice turns hoarse and I can feel the rawness in my own throat.

Come, Mama. Mama, coooooome.

She slept fine on her own for so long. I don't understand where this new resistance is coming from. Some restlessness related to diet—too much lobster bringing the commotion of the sea into her body?—or is it real fear, related to something she's come, finally, to understand, just when it's almost over? Just when everything's about to be fine. I'm determined to let her cry it out. To just sit here, in agony, until she's exhausted herself to the point of sleep.

Mama!

Paul puts his hand on my leg. I haven't moved, but he must sense my muscles preparing, must see that every cell in my body is agitating, wanting to go to her, to make everything, immediately, okay. To feel the rush of okayness.

My agitation, for the moment, coalesces around his fingertips on my thigh.

It's how I feel every second.

Which is more than he's said about it, in all these weeks and months. These two and a half years. And for a second it's like it's my husband beside me, someone I know; it's like a deep, sinking relief, for every part of me except my thigh, which is so fucking tense. I take deep breaths and try to relax the muscle. To soften. To not be so horribly obdurate.

You can get a fearful horse to bow her head—to be vulnerable—with a two-handed method. With one hand, squeeze behind her ears to release the tension there. When the good feeling gets her to lower her head an inch, use your other hand to create a new ceiling for it. Squeeze, lower the ceiling. Squeeze, lower the ceiling. We called the squeeze an ask.

Ask, release. Ask, release. Ask, release. My hand is over his on my thigh.

The house goes quiet.

EXERCISE

The madman is missing. *Der irrer fehlt.*

The missing husband may arrive. *Der vermisste Ehemann kann eintreffen.*

The chance to know the mother was missed. *Die Chance, die Mutter kennenzulernen, wurde verpasst.*

Nothing useful, nothing useful, nothing useful. No emails, no answers, no solutions. Nothing to do but wait. Stick with the faith that's been chosen.

Der Insel fehlt der Bruder, dessen Gesicht ihre Finger kannten. (The island is missing the brother whose face her fingers knew.)

I watch him step into the oilskins, as the boat pulls away from the dock. Like he's stepping into himself. When he returns, he hangs the skins at the door.

We share the house but move in different worlds.

BEND

I have to try. Give him something to return to.

His hair is now long and thick, more golden than I've ever seen it from his time on the water. I squeeze the washcloth, with its pattern of blue irises, over his head. I use it to scrub his skin, everything above the waist, with vinegar. What I'm trying to scrub out is beneath the fish, too, though he doesn't know it.

I smell it, I've noticed, when I start to feel hopeful.

The tiger.

I smell it while he sleeps off the labor of the day—sprawled on top of the covers before dinner. Open-mouthed, unaware. Dreaming whatever he dreams.

He has no internet. No way of getting to a mailbox. No means of procuring money orders. He's always with Sharon. He doesn't set foot on land.

Agnes, sitting on the toilet, thinks this bath is funny. I suspect he's frustrated by her presence—unsure what to do with himself.

The circles I'm making are getting tighter and rougher. This isn't turning out like I hoped.

What do you want? His voice is careful and tender.

It's fine, I say. I drop the washcloth into the water.

Agnes is right behind me. What is it, Mama? Why that face?

•

What if it's me who's irretrievable? The one who's gone?

It's funny to think of sanity this way: like a sheet, hanging from the line. On one side, the magical thinking. And on the other, the paranoia. The sheet billows. The sheet is porous—it lets a little of each side through; it must. It's a thing of give and take, of bend and manage. The key is to not be overtaken by the forces on either side. It must take whatever shape it must, second by second. Make any contortion. Whatever it takes to stay out of the dirt.

The key for that sheet is to not become too stiff. Too unyielding.

The key for that sheet is to not let salt and sun leave it parched and hardened.

I'm thinking that maybe ritual can help.

I pour baking soda onto my grandmother's washcloth this time, a dab of the vinegar, and make nice, loose circles as I scrub.

Let's cut your hair, I say. I want to see his familiar head, the shape of it.

Okay, he says. Because on this day, again, he's willing to do what it takes. To sit here, and try to be what I need.

I leave and return with scissors.

He's looking at me like someone who loves me and is sorry.

His hair is floating all about him in the tub.

What I want so badly now is my phone. To see the old pictures. To be able to say, yes, that really is him.

In my memories, he's faceless. It can't be this one. There must have been something different, before.

I look away. I smile.

But he's smarter than that.

I've prepared myself this time.

> *Have met the most incredible woman with a hostel and chickens. You wouldn't believe these eggs. No WWW with her, but this town is not too far and we have to come sometimes for Nescafe and toilet paper for the rooms. She would like to see the States and even meet you and your brother someday but for now business is busy. Will write again when I can. You pay by the minute here. You can handle the lawyers.*

No, Dad, I type. *They need you.* I need you. You fucker. But Jesus. It's Dad. It's my very own dad.

The important thing, it seems, is to delete the email. In lieu of a real return, what needs to be established is absence. For *missing* to hit its legal mark.

But that absence needs to exist for five years, the statute says. I already flaunted his first email before the executor. Can I argue I've come to believe it a hoax?

•

Imagine being not a child in love with him, but a wife.

Now they won't stop coming:

> *Whatever they're telling you it's not true. They have in-*
> *terests in the stars and in carbons that they think they*
> *can get to through me but this isn't true. This is the only*
> *place I am safe so don't let them fool you.*

Mescal? Coke? Just too much sun? Dehydration?
He never even drank, before. He had his theories. TV,
beer—it was all designed to subdue.
Delete.

How long did it take for the ground to feel firm and steady and
familiar beneath Mom's feet? When she moved from his world
to one she could share with everyone else.

FADE

In the spring, the horses would eat the raspberries that grew around the edge of the field, then roll across the ground in pain. My mother and I would coax them up onto their feet and walk them around in the short grass until our minds had wandered far from what we were doing and the horses' pain had eased, until my mom no longer knew I was there behind her.

It was this power to go unseen that enabled me to stay so close. If I'd spoken, I would likely have been sent back to the house.

REPEAT

It's throaty, quick, almost like the bark of a seal. Sharon's laugh. What has he said? They're out past the ledge. He's in his skins.

I might murder someone, to feel the weight of a bottle on my stomach.

Or maybe I'm wrong. Maybe it was a seal.

On the dash—if it's called a dash—there was a thermos, and two tin cups. It dawned on me: They have rituals. It dawned on me: Those skins once belonged to somebody else.

She looks at me, or I look at her. Always theft—glances taken on the down low. It's like a full burning, either way. The humiliation of being seen. The power of seeing.

It's the hardest place, the intertidal zone. So says one of my grandmother's books. You need to not drown and you need to not dry up. It takes a special type. On long hot afternoons in the sun, hours out from the slow creep of the tide, snails seal up their opercula to keep their moisture in. Opercula. Head holes.

Elsewhere in the world, lungfish survive droughts by coating themselves in mud and sinking deep into sleep, the mud hardening and cracking in the sun until finally water returns and sets everything loose again, brings movement back to earth, and fish.

Lungfish can go three and a half years without food.

REPEAT

Again.

What's the difference between a dirty bus stop and a lobster with tits? I say.

I hold the washcloth at the base of his neck. I filled the bucket in the morning, soon after the *Rodney-Duane* carried him off, and left it in the sun to warm. It's August now, and the days are reliably hot.

Remind me.

One's a crusty bus station, the other's a busty crustacean.

It's more groan than laugh—he really had forgotten—but not bad. Probably not quite good enough to produce a chemical reaction in his brain, a reward.

How does a lobster answer the phone? I say.

Tell me.

Shello! And you do know where fishes go to work, right? I wait a beat, then give it to him. *The offish!*

You test those out on Agnes?

He's looking down at his arms, at the visible striations of fish oil lifting off his naked body. But he's smiling a little bit, I can tell.

I did, I say. I think the problem was, she doesn't know what a phone is. Or an office.

What I'm thinking, now, is that she thinks an office is the back of a car. Which he knows I'm thinking.

Knock, knock.
Who's there?
Boo.
Boo who?
You don't have to cry about it.

The others, in school, could size up a placenta in seconds. Could say with confidence that all was right. No pieces missing, everything just the right rosy color, no intervention necessary. Could stretch the bloody mass on the ground of the foaling barn until it looked like a five-year-old's drawing of a horse, or an ink spill, or whatever you might see, and say, Yep, all good.

I could spot a problem—a missing chunk, a meconium stain; that was easy. What I could not spot, with any confidence, was the lack of problem. If any little piece was missing, the mare could die of infection. How could you not just stand there, eyes roving, searching, unsure?

With the scissors, I lop off the hair that straggles below my chin.

HEART

TRASH

Agnes and I walk the high-tide line, dragging along behind us a giant translucent bag. The bag itself washed up; it's what gave us the idea. There are four categories of trash on this beach: empty Clorox bottles, Gatorade bottles (empty or full of pee), single flip-flops, and other. We're custodians.

I scan the far-out water, squinting against the sun, and pick out Sharon's buoys. Beneath them, all our hope. Beneath them, all our future. Tied to the end of a rope. I stare at the buoys hard, until it feels like I'm moving, until they disappear into the bright light, and I lower my eyes to the beach and can see again, and bend to extract an orange flip-flop with a snapped thong that's sticking halfway out of the sand.

Agnes insists I try it on.

I have no idea why, sometimes, I try to resist her will. It just prolongs things. She always wins in the end.

The rubber, between my toes, feels alarmingly intimate. I shake this other person's thing off my foot.

We're down on the dock when they come back. I've thrown the giant trash bag full of bleach bottles into the dory. I've sorted the Gatorade bottles into a separate bucket, having stood ankle-deep in the incoming tide and dumped the sun-warmed piss of strangers into the ocean.

The Clorox labels show through the thin plastic.

Shame how being a fucker one way makes you a fucker another way, too, Sharon says.

She doesn't mean me, I don't think. I'm not the fucker. I nod, but I doubt she notices—she's back to spraying water across the deck of her boat, sending bits of guts scurrying out the little hole in the stern.

Agnes is rapt.

It was quick but I saw it. Sharon's eyes leaving Agnes. I saw that she had to turn her head. That she was unprepared for something. That she has not avoided the child, thus far, for lack of feeling.

There's Paul, coiling ropes. Not looking up to help me understand the comment. As he would have, if he were really Paul. Instantly knowing when I was lost.

He looks good though, actually. His face and body carry the strangeness—the darkness of the flesh beneath his eyes, the starkness in the angles of his face, the lost confidence in the way he uses his body—but also something fresh. A blankness. An openness one finds on the face of a child that wants to please. It feels a bit cruel to study him this way.

I should give them this time. I should stop standing here, intruding. I should let her bring him out.

I should stop thinking it matters which one of us does it.

I lift the bag with the bleach bottles into the dumpster behind the supermarket. Inside, I let Agnes feed the redeemables into the machine. We listen as our new dollar and sixty-five cents tinkles down into the little chamber.

She smiles. She seems to understand, preternaturally, that this is a sound of well-being.

When I was a child—sixth grade—I hid from the world the fact that I was God.

We make our rounds, collecting our scraps from the kits.

That year, I was come to earth, in that meek human form, to Watch and to See. How long did it last? Weeks? A year?

Such a strange child, like all of them.

You ignore a thing long enough, and it disappears.

Was Rodney-Duane a little thing, just the size of Agnes?

I know his hands are too tired from the day's work to help me scrape these barnacles off—and besides, there's just the one knife that's good for this. To keep him in the kitchen, I ask what Sharon meant. I remind him of the bleach bottles, her comment.

It's illegal to keep lobsters that have eggs attached, he says. Some guys bleach them off.

I add a clean mussel to the pile. Maybe tonight, again, Agnes will crush a tiny pearl between her teeth. Too small to be of any value; a private gem.

It's pretty fucking stupid, he continues. They just want the money. They don't care about what anyone will do down the road.

The shell drops away from my knife.

What? he says, looking back at me.

And I think it would be better if he left the room. Before my fury drags him back to hell. Before I clobber him over the head with the mace of everything he's done. Which isn't my aim tonight.

CONUNDRUM

Who's Rodney-Duane? I ask. So casually.
   Paul shrugs and doesn't look up from his plate.
   You don't know?
   Not really, he says. Still not looking up.
   There's a reason I stopped asking questions.

How lovely, to just be out there on the water, shooting the breeze all day.
   It's hard to know how you feel about the woman who's saving your husband.

GOD OF SIGHT

Seeing is half the battle.

Seeing half is the battle.

But there's more.

Her wedding ring waits in a tin can inside her kitchen door, the bottom of which is darkened by smudges—from dirty boots and noses. There are two big dogs inside to greet her, in love with the smell of her. Enraptured. A voice from another room—wanting, expectant. The voice of a child that has not grown up. That won't rise from the couch. That she's too scared to chase away. There's no one attached to the ring anymore, but she still puts it on. She can't deal with this child alone.

Maybe it's not a can. Maybe it waits in the cup holder of her truck. She starts the engine, adjusts the radio, slips it on. Still married to something. An idea of herself. It's "Jumpin' Jack Flash." She turns it up.

She's invited Agnes onto her boat—the first time she's addressed her, directly, in all these weeks. I've come aboard, behind Agnes, who did not let go of my shirt.

She's showing her how to keep hold of one of the slippery creatures from the tub as its strong tail pumps, up and down, as its useless claws go wild. Agnes is focused. Nervous, but undeterred. There's a curved line of missing dark hairs on Sharon's forearm. A scar of something that gripped her. Otherwise, her arm hairs are bushy. Wild.

Agnes's body is loosening. She holds the thing a good two seconds before it breaks free and smacks the deck of the boat. She sees it as success. For two seconds, it was her and the beast, and she was winning.

She was alone when it happened. When the throttle jammed and the rope caught her arm and kept her pinned, in the water, against the hull of her boat, until it broke free.

She wasn't supposed to be alone. The child should have been with her.

He got his own license when he was twelve. She started paying him when he was fourteen. She would, eventually, have given him the boat. There was no one to talk it over with. No one to tell: I had to change the locks. No one to hear her say: He beat on every window and I threw up in the closet, hiding.

The dogs had been distraught when he got in, lowering a foot to the floor. Had growled and whined, had licked his hand with tails between their legs. Hadn't stopped him from taking any of it, what was left. Her tower of CDs. A platter her father had brought home from Japan. His uniform.

Did she even know you're supposed to keep scars out of the sun?

Yes. But there was supposed to be someone else to remind her.

La-diddy-da-diddy-da-diddy-do.
A voice from before.
A wife.

It's easy, once you get going. Seeing what no one knows you can see.

WANT

It's more important that she like him, I know. For our survival. She can think I'm all dried up. An unfit mother. A complete dolt of a human being. It wouldn't matter.

But fuck. How unfair.

He gets to have a friend.

Try as I might, I can't see what they're like out there.

AWAKE

I watch him sleeping in the bed next to me. I can smell the fish, of course. Feel tender, I think. *Feel tender, feel tender, feel tender.*

When he opens his eyes I say, What did the dead fish juice say to the fisherman?

Mmuh, he says.

Take me home to your wife.

Sorry, he says, and rolls back over into sleep.

The work is good for him if for no other reason than it makes him sleep.

I walk around the house with the $1,600 in my hand, looking for a new place to put it.

For an apartment, we'll need $3,600.

I've been wondering, so I ask. *Do humans have an operculum?* I type. Not *Do humans have anal glands*, or *Do humans have pheromones*, or *Do humans have tails*, as others have apparently wondered.

The answer is yes. Several. In our brains. They begin developing in fetuses at about twenty weeks. Little lids to protect their *insula*—their little island, their little private piece of brain.

And finally! They're here.

I watch as Agnes reaches deep into the rosebush again, trying to figure out how to extract a particularly bright red hip, a tight little bud, from through all the yellowing leaves and black-tipped thorns, without getting scratches on her face.

You know what else, kiddo? I say. We can eat them with our teeth.

There are thin scratches up and down her arms, droplets of blood as tiny as the grit-like pearls.

Her face twists, her body shivers. She grins and takes a second sour, chalky bite. The seeds splay out on her tongue. By nature, she takes what she can. A different sort of god than me.

We cut the hips in half and spread them in the sun.

I sit up and it's dark.

I've been dreaming of aborted foals—glistening red sacs dropping from the vulvas of every mare in the barn, one after the other, as soon as my eyes settled on them. The mares' eyes were wide; they thrashed their heads. I was holding a syringe, looking for a horse I could still vaccinate against this problem. But my eyes were the problem. My eyes were causing the abortions.

COMMUNION

Agnes is pounding on the keyboard of the empty computer next to mine. I grab her hands to stop her and she screams. The other computerists look at us.

I log out and scoop her up. She screams louder and kicks her legs.

As I'm turning around, an old man clasps my elbow, gently, like he's been expecting this meeting, and holds it while he looks from me to Agnes. Agnes, amazingly, quiets. He exhales and his warm booziness enters our circle. This gentle touch, this intimate aroma.

I had a dream last night, he says, that my mother was pregnant. At eighty years old, if you can you believe it.

I wonder if he's noticed that my skin has gone up in goose bumps.

I couldn't get back to sleep after that. Just tossing, you know.

Hard to shake, I agree, hoping he won't walk away just yet.

I don't even know if my mom is *alive*, you know?

I nod.

How old do you think I am?

His light brown skin is rough and cracked, the pockets under his eyes discolored. I breathe in more of his smell.

Sixty-two.

That old? Oh, man.

Fifty-seven, I say.

Yes, that's it. Fifty-seven.

He walks away. He seems to be very content, to have been reminded of his age.

Agnes, for the next hour, is mellow and cooperative. As if in a trance, like me.

We go by a church with its message board stating: *If He Puts Us In Darkness, It Is So We Can Seek Out His Light.* The church has a lot to explain, these days.

It's a thing I could do. Go to a church. Sit among strangers while they sing. It wouldn't cost a penny, aside from gas. But would it be wrong? To claim that closeness? The brush of others' arms, the vibrations of their songs? Would it be a kind of theft to sit among them, pretending?

What if I dreamed about my mother?

Fuck. I did not feed the meter. But it looks like we've all got them, tucked beneath our wipers.

We do not truly see light, we only see slower things lit by it, so that for us light is on the edge—the last thing we know before things become too swift for us. —C. S. Lewis.

I put it in my pocket. I turn to see where Agnes is.

Ka-thunk.

There's a sweater in the window there. The most beautiful gray wool. A little bell dings as we step inside. The wool is softer than I could ever have imagined. It's $268.

I do have that much, back in the can.

I try it on.

I do not want to take it off.

I take it off, hand it back to the woman, who must have seen my type before. I recompose. It would be odd to grab her and shake her, to scream. To tell her, in so many words: *I Just Want Fucking Something.*

She doesn't get paid enough.

I'm proud of you, I say, when he comes into the house. He's stepped out of his skins and hung them on the peg outside the kitchen door.

Nice of you to say so, he says. He does not meet my eyes. He does not smile. He shrugs my hand off his shoulder and peels off his horrible socks. First nice thing in twelve days.

You have, what, a *diary*? I say.

I'm treated to his back moving down the hall, toward the bathroom.

Before he gives me the money.

What the fuck was that?

I put the $70 I find later on the table into my sock and later, when I'm sure he's sleeping, cross the long grass to the shed and turn on my flashlight and unscrew the cap to the oil can, and let the fattening scroll of bills, held tightly by a thick purple rubber band, slide out. I lay them all flat, adding my new bills, and count them again: $1,840. It's just now September. I've bought a few things. Like the pizza loaded with fake meat. Fuel.

Is there a way to confirm the amount with Sharon, without letting her see us for what we actually are?

I felt my way through, my palms hitting flank and tail. Tripping, occasionally, over what was lost. Glistening red on the ground. Don't look, I kept telling myself. Don't look and it will all be fine. In the dream.

But $70 is still a lot. Far more than the kits bring in.

I woke up crying. No nose. No cheekbones. No lips. Just flank after flank after flank.

Should I buy the sweater *now*, before I tighten up again, our deadline unignorable? Before I know what's happening? When I might still be considered innocent?

The thing about the familiar is that it can go unnoticed.

But he doesn't go ashore.

DELICACIES

There's a hand of it in this night, a backside, like air just let up from a cellar. I let it feel my face as I stand in the grass, then sit, looking up at what stars there are to see, the planets and things I've never known the names of.

Woodcocks, we learned back in Pittsburgh, spend their days protected by forest thickets. But at night, to sleep, they seek out open places. Pastures, abandoned fields. Places of no protection.

Maybe they see no reason for their surrender to be anything but complete.

Maybe they have no concept of ever waking up again.

Maybe they don't have $1,840 in a can, for tomorrow.

Maybe there was no avoiding it; he's gained the upper hand. I take the money I'm given.

Agnes goes to bed with Paul, her backside against his stomach. I wonder to what extent this is what he's always wanted—this constant company, this mutual adoration—and to what extent she's a useful fortress.

I watch Agnes cross the line that I cannot.

•

He gives me the money when he thinks of it, or when I ask for it, later, gently.

With each sum I perform a recalculation—how much do we need him to bring home on each remaining day?

But you exist within capitalism, I heard my mother saying. How do you think being anti-capitalist is helping you? How is that working?

That wasn't too long before the bumper stickers, actually. I don't think.

They could have been a gesture, of sorts. A foray. An effort. Or maybe they were only ever meant to drive her crazy. To show her what a monster she was. What she wanted him to be, for the sake of money.

I've built a fire and am sitting in front of it, little scraps of paper all around me. I can't see as well as I need to, but I won't turn on another light. The fire itself is a waste; we'll miss this wood before too long.

I arrange and rearrange the scraps, waiting for an argument to rise up. I hold the phrases in my head. The word itself, *legalese*, becomes abstract, separated from its meaning. It strikes me as something that should be eaten off fine china, picked apart with pretty forks. Perhaps served with a stemmed glass of something very dry and red.

At dinner, she asked, so I told her. It's everywhere, I said. Referring to the heart. It's all of it. She paused for a moment before jabbing her little fingers into the mess, pulling a slippery hunk of everything from the hard red shell, and eating it.

What is that *face*, I ask her. She looks holy, euphoric.

I'm loving her babies for her. Since she's inside me.

God of Voracity. God of Benificence.

I count what I've brought home in my pocket, making a little pile on the bed. A mound of coins sliding toward the weight of my body. A mound with a smell that stays on my fingers.

I'm late to the dock—have come to see what the holdup is. I sent her down in her life vest to bring her father up. To welcome him home.

Sharon's got her arm around her as they cast and pull in a fishing line, as they pry yet another feisty crab off the end of it—where it clings, of its own stubborn accord, to a scrap of bait. Paul's busy with something in the front of the boat. They drop the crab into a bucket by their feet. Agnes, at ease in the scoop of that arm.

I see how quickly she reestablishes distance when she sees me seeing them. How she pulls away from my child. The slide of a foot. The turn of a torso.

Sharon's nice, huh?

Agnes nods.

What is it you like about her?
Her hands.
A little funny, right?
She looks at me doubtfully.
Papa told you?
Told me what?
She shakes her head. I'm not supposed to tell.
Agnes, what?! It's not okay to have secrets!
She's magic.
Oh. What else?
She has twin engines. Born at the exact same time.

Where is she taking them? My family? Why am I the only one who cannot come?

If she was magic, I didn't say, she'd still have Rodney-Duane.

From nowhere, it drives me crazy.
  Why is your nose so drippy? I say. You've been like that for weeks.
  Not that I was expecting an answer. Anything but this look, which shows me what I've become.

It's not exactly the tiger.
  The smell that evades me, more and more. The closer we get.
  It's the tiger and some other things. The coins from my

fingers, the vinegar from the baths. These smells that return and don't recede, that exist in places that don't make sense— pockets behind the shed, clouds along the shore. A stale curtain in the closet of Agnes's room. I don't know what's on the outside, and what's carried in my nostrils, memories that won't wash out.

All of it, every bit, obscured by fish, the harder I try to follow.

PETITION

I stand in the line at the post office to buy a stamp.

My petition is real, official, the phrases pulled from my head and typed up and printed on computer paper, stapled to a form I completed with the date and appropriate check marks and my name, printed and signed.

The easy part goes like this:

> *If a person entitled to or having an interest in property has disappeared or absconded from the place within or without the State where he was last known to be, and has no agent in the State, and it is not known where he is, or if such person, having a spouse or minor child dependent to any extent upon him for support, has thus disappeared or absconded without making sufficient provision for such support, and it is not known where he is, or, if it is known that he is without the State, anyone who would under the law of the State be entitled to administer upon the estate of such absentee if he were deceased, may file a petition under oath in the probate court, praying that such property may be taken possession of.*

Walking away from the post office, I can swear I see Paul, at the far end of my sight.

Walking back to our car, I see the sweater is gone from the shop window. Someone has the same wants as me. I wonder if shame is ruining her pleasure. I wonder how long she'll wear it.

VISION

Maybe we can do it.

Stay.

Eat snow.

Get out in the night and poach lobsters. Put our money not in some landlord's hands, but into a fleet of propane tanks, hot water bottles, a wet suit for each of us. Base layers from Patagonia.

We should have been chopping and drying wood all along. The woodshed is nearly empty.

I count the money again.

Imagine her knees drawn up to her chest. Frozen crystals forming in the tissues of her arms and legs, her cheeks, as her body shuttles blood instead to her vital organs. Brain, heart, lungs, liver, kidneys. Which does it give up on first?

I put the bills in my sock, until later.

Imagine being just short.

The tiger, at least, was warm. Was attended by heat. These other things are like cold fingers. The smell of chemicals, a lab, of a coroner gowned up and ready to go. Pennies with frothy green crust.

RE-VISION

Paul's gone up to the shed, to see what gas we have. They worked against a wind all day, and Sharon is low, though she insisted she's fine. Which of us is more uncomfortable, without Paul there between us? Which of us has a question we're willing to ask, now that we find ourselves here?

Sharon—

She doesn't unbend. Doesn't stop sorting.

There's an explanation; she wouldn't ignore me. Her hearing isn't what it should be. An infection of her right eardrum when she was a child, from spending too much time in the water, swimming in wide circles with a big black Lab I can see as clear as day. Paul has learned to work around it, the handicap—to come at her from the left. Or maybe they don't need words by now; their bodies say what they need. They communicate in gestures.

I don't know how to begin. Does he seem good, my husband? Like someone it's good to be married to? I wish I could say this, in gesture. Without giving anything away.

Sharon—

The tide's up high, the water dark.

Agnes keeps squirming free of my fingers, wanting to be on her own, to run to the edge of the dock. She's not wearing her life jacket. For all her bravado, she has not learned how to swim. I grab her wrist; she twists it. I hold more tightly; she shouts and tries to pull away. I pick her up and she screams in my face. What she has never imagined is her body disappearing into that darkness.

Sharon's looking at me. Now. At us. This little stir. I see that she's unbent now, and facing us, the headphones over her ears.

I move my eyes to the fish in the bucket.

The internet showed me a video of a lobster heart beating. A woman had drilled through the animal's shell and glued over the square-inch absence a piece of clear plastic. A neat little window. Agnes's wrist is in my grip.

My eyes move to the holding tank. My heart. The fish.

Sharon—where are the lobsters?

What's that? She slides the headphones so they encircle her neck.

Where are the lobsters?

The pound, she says.

The floor of my chest—it went where? There are so many types of ground, to fall away.

She hauls up an engine, unwinds a thick strand of rockweed from the propeller. Like it's the same world she was in a second ago.

Paul comes down with just a hose, hops into the dory.

Nah, she says. I'll make it. I should make it.

I wasn't expecting the wind. This she says to me.

The pound. Ashore.

Just a little, Paul says. Unscrewing the gas cap. Putting his mouth to the end of the hose.

DANCE

Agnes is holding two pieces of bright red discarded shell—a tail and a claw. She's making them dance on the table.

You want me to tell her I can't help her with that? That my wife says I can't go ashore? That she needs to power ten miles out of her way to drop me here first?

Do I?

Rodney was a husband. Duane's the son. I'm trying this on. They're both gone—for reasons I don't yet know. What else I don't know is whether they love her, the way she loves them. Enough to name her boat for them. Not enough to follow. To Massachusetts; to New Brunswick; to a new life Born Again, a wide field and a slumped little church; to a dead mother's trailer on the lake, on the county road he grew up on; to the bottom of the sea.

She's here. They're not.

I pull up Craigslist to see what's changed. Still twelve hundred to go for a very shitty apartment.

References will be tricky. Furniture, of course, can wait. We'll all need coats, and boots.

Between the library and the car is a big stone church, with the doors wide open. Agnes wants to hear the singing, though I've tried to shuffle us past. It's embarrassing, when she screams in public. When people turn to watch.

We listen.

It seems that there's a balm in Gilead.

Did you know?

You may be filled, O hungry one, the table's spread for you.

At the store, she reaches for a box of cookies. No, I say, taking it gently. She reaches for a container of premade potato salad. No, I say, prying it from her hands. She reaches, as I know she will, for one of the chickens.

What is it I'm looking for? We leave with a bag of rice and five cans of beans.

We have twenty-one days.

Today he brought home $40.

Is it normal? I said. This time of year?

Water's fished out.

He brings home nothing.

We have nineteen days.

I'll be sure to tell the lobsters, he says.

He's even short with Agnes. I know I shouldn't be this happy she's taken my hand. That she's whispering into my ear. Let's go, Mama, away from Papa. Let's just be us.

•

I could have said more or less. Nineteen days, *more or less*. Until the weather might easily turn us into the parents of headlines. Of even grosser negligence. Involuntary manslaughter. Toddlerslaughter! I could imagine the way my face would droop in the picture, skin with no more reason to hang on.

Each extra day a gamble.

He brings home $50.

Mom said we had no place taking in horses.

But when Dad arrived towing a rented trailer, and we coaxed the two old mares out of it, she said nothing. Once we'd gotten them lodged in the barn that had slouched unused on the property all my life, she brought them apples. I watched her and wanted to feed them, too, to know what their giant horse lips would feel like against my palm.

Someone had been about to turn them into glue. I knew that's what she was thinking about.

Eventually, when the kits came into our lives, I made her a sticker: HORSES ARE THE GLUE THAT BINDS US. I gave it to her by placing it on the back of her old green Rabbit. I could tell from the corners of the orange vinyl that she tried to peel it off.

It had made sense to me then, at age eleven. I thought it would be the perfect thing.

My mother, taking notice of me once, said the horses dreamed only when they were like this—lying down, their ears twitching, flank muscles jerking; that the lock-kneed standing sleep was neither here nor there.

They have to be totally gone to be with us again, she said. Watch—see how she takes the apple from my palm?

In its dream, she meant.

Agnes's cheeks are twitching. Her hand gives a quick little flop, like a fish jumping out of the water.

HEAD

CATHEDRAL

At the time, it had been unthinkable.

The cedars had formed a cathedral in front of the house. We would sit on the porch and listen to the birds in the high canopy, as my grandmother named them by their calls. We'd watch the shadows shift among the leaves. And then, one summer, they were gone. We showed up and there were the charred remains. It entered through the wounds, she said— great silvery streaks. She'd had them felled and burned. She almost never brought anyone over, to do anything.

Dad was still raw from Mom's disappearance. Conrad and I were still doing kid stuff and knowing it was wrong of us.

I lurked through the shadows of the house, sticking to the parts that remained unchanged, and listened to my grandmother talking to my father on the porch, past which there was too much bright, blaring open sky. When we arrived, she'd handed him a little glass of brandy before he even set his duffel bag down on the kitchen floor. Which was as far as she would go in bringing it up. My mother's disappearance. He touched the glass to his lips and set it down, full, on the table.

He left us there for the rest of the summer, got us back to school a week late.

When I went out of the house, I kept my eyes closed until I was safely past, until there were trees all around me.

For suppers, she made us brown bread with giant slabs of

butter, corn on the cob with giant slabs of butter, fresh summer zucchini stewed with butter, tomatoes, and thyme. I picked the sausage out of my own.

Now sunlight kisses the crowns of the spruces that have made a claim on the soil, the undulating fronds of ferns, the fire-weed I'll sauté in the spring, when the shoots are young, if *missing* is interpreted in my favor.

Wants, too, sneak in, from somewhere.

The silvery gashes grew, until there was no turning back.

Where did his pain get in, in the first place? How does it enter? Is it happening to her, right now?

Other kids, I knew, had Cheetos and Jell-O pudding for lunch. Ham sandwiches slickened with mayonnaise for dinner. Mom took what we had and turned it into slow-simmered stews with herbs she grew, bright pink borscht, daal thickened with cheese she strained through a cloth.

For the first time, it hits me: She didn't have to.

CHILL

I feel it first in the tip of my nose. I sit up and a small amount of snot drips like water from my nostril onto the mauve wool blanket, eaten through in places by moths.

Paul is out on the water. The rope will be sliding through his unfeeling fingers, the excess water sloughing off as the rope passes through the cradle of his thumb. In a few hours, his fingers won't bend. Will hardly be able to work the latches of the cages that contain, I must hope, more than a couple of lobsters.

I've got to try. I can't be such a monster.

I draw a warm bath, despite how low we are on the propane that heats the water in the pipes. I'll cut my portions in half this week. Rely more on seaweed. We won't drive anywhere that's not entirely necessary. We'll walk as much as we can.

Going off the dock, he says.

Aren't you sick of that ocean yet?

We'll join you, I say, when he keeps on going. A towel over his shoulder.

God forbid you let me out of your sight.

So we don't. Join him. So we do. Let him out of our sight.

Apple! I say. Where were we hiding all this?

Our water is full of detritus. But warm.

We need another bath to clean up from this one!

She thinks it's even funnier than I do.

I climb out quickly, towel off, and re-dress. I have this feeling he might be returning. That he might see me taking more than I need.

I feel his approach, reassembling me.

I make a fire in the kitchen stove. I go to the shed and check the can. We have $2,145.86. I have a mother cat's instinct to move it. If I put it in the woodpile it might get burned up. If I put it in the earth it might get wrecked by moisture. If I put it in the house somewhere—I once heard of a man whose life savings, at the back of a drawer, were shredded by a single mouse.

I leave the money in the can.

GOD OF ADMINISTRATION

What comes, in addition to the chill, is an email. Letting me know, as a courtesy, that after taking his fees, there is not enough left in the estate to continue making payments on the taxes. That in the interests of his fiduciary obligation to my grandmother, his intention is to sell the property in the spring, before it's seized and auctioned by the county, and to manage the monetary assets gained by such sale until such time as my father comes to claim them. He is offering me the first chance at a private sale before he lists the property publicly.

If those woodcock boys had to put on suits and report to jobs, I wonder what they could come to love. Instead of spiraling flight.

TANG

I go to look for mussels, now that the tide is out. It's the crabs, I've learned—the green ones, which have come down from Nova Scotia—that have caused the dearth of them. Eating the babies, when their shells are soft and useless. Every last one, until they're gone.

They think it's the warmer water causing the spike of aggression. The utter lack of self-control.

I bring back a bucket brimming with bladder wrack.

He welcomes her, if not me.

Before them: a pile of crumpled-up magazine pages, a few long spaghetti boxes twisted into something like rawhides, a scattering of little sticks, a few small logs from what we've got left.

He's home again because of the weather. Because of this cold, steady drizzle. Sharon's too old to bother, when the fishing's bad. That's what Paul says.

She can't call, so each morning he goes down to the dock, ready.

Agnes is in his lap, gripping the cuff of his pant leg with one of her fists.

They assemble and disassemble the components in the middle of the rug. He critiques each of their constructions, praising oxygen channels, progressive denseness, shapeliness. This one's like a temple, I hear him say.

I know it's a thing people do. The believers. Bend over backward to explain the sudden absence.

Twenty-five percent of drug addicts recover. His addiction was barely real. *Krah-tm.* A fake word.

Have I imagined everything?

There's a package of cotton swabs in the medicine cabinet. From about 1972, I'd guess. I use one to scrub my nostrils.

Maybe I'm just being tested. Maybe someone has plans for me.

Three days since he's been out. Three days of foul weather. Three days of no money. I'm almost as surprised as I am distraught. He's sleeping at midday again and she wants to stay with him.

When I return, she's lined him with periwinkle shells. With the snakeskins and bird bones, from the windowsill.

Why are you scratching like that?

He takes his hand from his throat, which is red. He starts on his wrist, where it juts from below his sleeve.

Do you have a rash?

He looks at his fully clothed body.

No? he says. He's hardly awake yet. The salt, it irritates.
You're still congested.

He waits for whatever's next.

Are you sick? Can I help?

The rain is cold, and sideways. Still, I sit on the rocks to scrape
the shells, rather than taking them back to the house. I can't be
in the house. With all his sleeping.

The handle is slippery, my fingers red. I push harder, my
thumb steering the blade into the base of a dangerously sharp
barnacle. I do something two-handed, weird, and the handle
splits. The two pieces of wood fall away, giving up the blade—
tang, spine, tip, and all. Lying in my palm. The clean silver
tang and the rust-pocked blade.

Agnes doesn't look at me; I think she's seen. She's tracing
the length of stiff green rope that's tangled in the rockweed
as the rain pelts the trash bag that's covering her, her head
poking out through the man-made hole, the wind sending the
black plastic back toward the trees; this one's coming in from
the north. She's talking to herself, I can see. We shouldn't have
lost that Rumpelstiltskin.

I add the pieces of the knife to the pile of shells in my
bucket.

Thirteen mussels, plus the jam I made from the rose hips,
spread on Wonder Bread.

Tea, too, to stave off colds.

See this, Mom. I could be doing worse.

•

Here's what I've been given. Maybe I should give myself back. Just lie on the beach in the rain with these gifts in my stomach, let whatever happens happen. Let the world take care of me.

The rain stops. I wake Paul at the sound of her boat.

The ferns go gold at the tips of their fronds. The gold bleeds inward, and the plants begin to lie flat; it looks like a dozen massive beasts bedded down for the night.

A few deep, sustained winds push the settled fog toward the sound, and bring the yellow leaves, with their minuscule teeth, to ground from the paper birches.

I stand still to notice it against my flesh, one last time—this air that has just a touch of warmth.

Maybe it's Sharon who has a plan for me.

There's one apartment that no one is taking. I'm not looking into why. The landlord wants $2,850—first, last, security. We need $560.

Which at this rate—

Will be a miracle.

•

I'd have lost it in a few weeks anyway, unless I decided to take it with me—to steal it. The scraping knife.

What I will take: Her apron. A few of the flannels. *The Black Prince*, if I haven't finished it. A towel for each of us. Blankets, including the one with the star. Things that won't be missed.

Agnes, I say. Looking into the drawer. What have we done with all the spoons?

The question is rhetorical—I'm sure I can find them under the couch, on the edge of the dresser, skimmed with the pale grime of Skippy and saliva—but off she goes, and then returns, with a silver bouquet.

Silly goose. Why were you keeping all those?

Ka-thunk.

Show me, I say.

She points to a dark corner, now empty, below the bathroom sink. Behind the plastic tub that keeps the toilet paper dry, when there's extra.

Silly spoons, I say. Telling secrets, I bet.

It's me who has this power: to become two things at once, so seamlessly.

Look! I say.

It's Rumpelstiltskin. Far back in the opposite corner. His yarn unraveling at his bottom edge.

Did you know he was here?

But she won't look at the puppet. She won't fucking play with this puppet, so I can tear through everything, all over again, unseen.

With two selves come two sets of wants and needs.

I do it casually, while she follows me.

Nothing.

A pocket full of gum wrappers. Two hundred and twenty-four of them. A wife, a mother, a granddaughter, a daughter. Smoothing and counting minty rectangles on wood engraved with reminders.

Maybe there's another explanation.

Notice: I haven't asked Agnes if she's cached the spoons. Haven't given her the chance to tell me no.

GOD OF FEAR, MISERLINESS, HOPE

I can see about twice as much of the lightening early dawn sky, through the trees, as a week ago. The leaves are slick and pretty underfoot.

I'm wrapped in one of the wool jackets, tan and red and boxy and scratchy, that my grandmother's husband used to wear—one of the ones I might take when we go. I'm there when the *Rodney-Duane* approaches.

Morning, she says. Her eyes coming up on me. Survive the rain?

No sense in waiting.

When you go to the pound—

But Paul's feet are heavy on the gangplank.

He gets in the boat like he's done five dozen times by now and casts them off, silently. I watch them get to work.

They pass the ledge, sending up a cormorant.

We settle on a banana for breakfast.

We thought hard about bowls of boiled kelp.

A tough choice.

Let's share one, I say, so there's more for later.

Imagine being within dollars of what we need. Within cents.

At least when he's out there, there's the possibility. Of $38 a day for the next twelve days. It's not impossible.

EYES

At the edge of the low gully, against the sea of ferns, the black pupils of little white berries pop in the fog, staring off in all directions. Beautiful and demented. The stalks are red and waxy. I'll have to look them up.

Agnes is behind me, straggling. She's made up with Rumpelstiltskin, so I'm back on the outside, a bit, while she mutters, then listens. Mutters, then listens.

Maybe you could do it: move away from a child whose need for you will end. Just quicken your step, before they leave your husk to blow where it might. Even in nature, it's frowned upon. Escaping your young. It was my mother who told me what the funnel-web spiders did behind our house. The ones that filled the grass. It's said that matriphagy is rare in nature, kept to just a few species. But that's the idea of men, she said. Men who haven't yet noticed how many ways a mother dies. They'll catch up.

I hear her first, then see her. Agnes, ten yards back, sitting on the damp blanket of leaves. Her cry a mix of hurt and fury.

She's still chewing when I get there, her tongue bearing the white mastication of the berries.

Agnes, no! I squeeze her cheeks to hold open her mouth.

Her cries grow sharper in pitch.

I scrape the mess off her tongue with my fingernails and pause: Rising from the pinkness are a few gentle welts, ringed with whitish scuzz.

We don't eat things we don't know, baby, I say, pulling her into me, hoping she knows I forgive her. That I'm not mad.

But her cries get wilder. I hold her shoulders and look her square in the face and try to make sense of it. What's wrong, Apple? The welts are now fiery, scarlet. Are they changing before my eyes? What next? Will they bubble over? She quiets. A few whimpers, then nothing. Her face is so pale. Isn't it pale? Where's Paul? Fishing. A terrible silence. I shake her shoulders. She looks so far away; she's looking at something so far away. What? Her eyes are glassy. I shake her harder. Agnes! Look at me!

I scoop her up; her body's so yielding—a pang of guilt accompanies the pleasure, the bodily recognition, the swift memory of her as a newborn, sleeping against my chest. Just after she was born, I sometimes had the urge to stuff her back in. To hold her on my inside, a little longer. There was a gorilla at a zoo who tried to do it. I read the headlines later. She crammed and crammed her infant against her lower parts, and it had to be taken away. It had to be nursed by humans then introduced, carefully, to a different female. Wake up, Apple!

We're at the dock. Somehow, we're at the dock, and I've grabbed the key from its place in the dirt, and I'm scrambling into the dory. Agnes is in my arms, and I'm pulling and pulling and pulling the choke. Goddamn my grandmother for having such a shitty boat. What was the point? I put Agnes on the damp slats between my feet. She won't even sit. I slide a life jacket beneath her head to keep it up. I do not scream out loud at the fucking piece-of-shit motor as I pull and pull and pull again until finally it catches. Goddamn my fucking girl arm. Goddamn Paul. We shouldn't be here. Goddamn my father.

What makes him think he deserves anyone's love? What makes him think it just waits? Good for my mom, for leaving. For just cutting him out. Conrad, I'm sorry. I shouldn't have left.

I leave the bumpers over and steer us through the fog, my eyes on the compass that's bolted to the bench, and on Agnes, and on the compass again, righting us. I pull Agnes into my lap—*come on, Apple*—then right our course again. I hold her to my chest and steer. Her face is hardly different from the fog—what if I lose her? Her eyes are closed. Her mouth a little open. Her head is tilted back. *You have to support the neck.* A thing someone could have told me. You hold them like *this*, feed them like *this*. Protect them, *this way*. To keep the pain from getting in. You could have left me with *something*, Mom.

I press my ear to her chest. I put my thumb to the soft flesh of her wrist, but my own heart is beating too fast. I let out my breath. I try again. I count. I shake her so maybe she'll open her eyes. Her lids flicker—still glassy. Water sprays from the dangling bumpers. Beyond the ledge the chop is stronger; we skip over a crest and land with a thud. Suddenly, vomit—shooting vomit that smells of real acids from her depths. Good girl. I should have thought of that; the horses ruined me. She cries—an innocent, infant-like cry. Good. The fucking fog; I yank the throttle, eyes back on the compass. I keep it at 240—straight shot from here, nothing in the way until the harbor. The boats begin appearing like ghosts in front of us. They rock in our wake. I throw a figure eight around a single cleat and leave the boat dangling. I climb out with Agnes clutched to my chest and clamber up the ramp. There's her screaming, there's this metal banging, there's this whiteness. At the top of the hill, I dig for my keys. Fucking Christ. This will do it. They're in here, right? Take me. Take all of me. Just give me my fucking keys. I feel them. Stop at a house to call an ambulance or straight to the hospital? I strap her into the car seat as fast as I can, her limbs limp, whatever fight had come back into her gone again. I won't stop. I won't stop to bang on an empty house.

I speed, and don't look at the gas gauge. Goddamn lying piece-of-shit Paul. If this car runs out of gas. She throws up again; I turn to make sure she's not choking on it. Good girl. I lean my seat back and reach as far as I can, tilt her head forward with my right hand while with my left hand I steer with my fingertips.

She left me Conrad.

Goddamn me, for all of it. For being so stupid. So irresponsible. For choosing blindness, when given eyes to see.

Even amid the relief, the nerves that catch up with me, making me shake, I take pride. Look at how her eyes shift around the room and take it all in, missing nothing. The humans in green scrubs who keep touching her, the beeping machines. She vomited once in the lobby, then again in this room.

They've taken her temperature. They've taken her blood pressure. They're monitoring her oxygen through a sticker taped to her toe. Her heart rate through stickers stuck to her chest. An IV for fluids? Only when the attending came, to try out different words, did I hear it right: They could do it to make me feel like a better mother. Not medically necessary. I hold the mask to her face as it puffs out the nebulized albuterol.

They give her apple juice. They give me apple juice, after seeing me take little sips of hers. She sleeps beautifully, for hours.

I watch her oxygen dance on the screen—98, 97, 99, 96, 98. Finally, I flip through the channels on the television until I find the little yellow creatures in the blue overalls. I wonder if, one day, this sort of thing will make any sense to her. If she'll be a part of this world.

They've observed her vitals behaving for six hours.

The nurse brings in the discharge papers. Earlier, he asked if we feel safe in our home.

Do you ever feel frightened in your home? he said, specifically.

Frightened? But I laughed to put him at ease. A good, three-semesters-of-vet-school laugh.

Do you always have enough to eat?

The girl who comes in from admitting knows.

She's seen us on the beaches. She's seen the half-rotten life vest, the shoe that was left too close to the fire, the milk that may have been bad because the propane ran out in the fridge. She knows, because she's not so far removed. But she has no power here.

Mail it, please, I say. In answer to her question.

The bill, I mean.

I've already given her my address—the house in Birdseye, that's been razed.

She knows. As good as knows.

Admit nothing, I whisper to Agnes, once we're alone.

I'm not ready to go back.

We go, instead, to the library. To see what's possible. But first, there's this:

You'd expect to feel their nails scratching at your scalp. But you don't. They're like the feet of angels. You just sort of wish they'd stay there forever. On your head, in your hair. You always wanted a monkey.

I hit delete.

I look up white baneberry. Nothing I didn't already learn from the toxicologist, whose gentle, paternal tone—the same one he used for all the mothers whose children ate paint chips or swallowed bleach—let me know that I was unequipped, but mercifully forgiven, because what was the alternative? All he could do was educate and hope for the best.

A few berries are enough to cause respiratory distress and even cardiac arrest—but are not usually swallowed, because of how horrible they taste.

The apartment's still listed, at the same price. Give it a few more weeks and it's possible the landlord will negotiate.

She's fallen asleep on my shoulder. My computer times out, but I stay.

At the grocery store, I get her everything she wants.

MACHETE

I thought I'd be rigid with anger. But sharing this—this enormous fright: I'm flooded. His arms are around both of us while I get it all out, the fear and regret and earth-smashing joy, while Agnes watches me. It feels like he'll never let go, that he's as relieved as I am to be back, to feel this love with me. Like we're here, a family. Like this was all we needed to snap back into ourselves, to love each other harder than we've loved anything, in a way that only we could. Here is our history. Here is us. Thank God.

Agnes does think it's odd. But also, I think, likes it. She looks at our faces. She does not ask why I look like this, but I know what she's thinking.

Because we love you so much, I whisper. I give her a tickle.

Is she hungry? Paul says. Will she eat? He's gone to the pantry, is looking for options, comes out holding the sack of potatoes. I'll make us some hash browns.

I don't tell him about the glistening chicken she had in the car. The juicy plum. The sticky handfuls of Honey Nut Cheerios.

I watch him at the stove.

We all eat, but mostly Agnes, from my lap. We slide potatoes from our plates to hers.

When there are just a few bites left on her plate, she stops. She looks at what's there.

Where's the heart? she says.

Here, I say, moving her from my lap to his. I'll wash up.

He sleeps on one side of her, while I lie awake on the other. But I must have finally fallen asleep, because I wake up just in time, and in just enough light, to see him disappearing into the woods with the machete gripped in his hands.

He thinks he's going to do what—cut it all down? Seek and destroy every last eyeball?

Still, I'll take it. This warm feeling I fold into myself, take with me back into sleep. I curl around Agnes.

He's new to this terror. The dailiness of it. He'll settle down. Give his protection more practically.

I hold my finger beneath her nostrils and hold my own breath until I feel her little heat on my skin, then relax again, settling into her slow rhythm.

It's been hours since I watched him head into the woods. His face is all scrambled around. He seems stuck in a bit of a hunch.

Got it all? I say. His back is turned now. He's what—working on the buttons of his jacket?

Paul! I say. Did you get it all? Trying to return my voice to normal.

I guess I'd better go to bed, he says.

He's nearly out of the kitchen before he stops.

Is Agnes okay?

Like he's just remembered.

There are floors you live unaware of. In your stomach, your

liver, your lungs. In each atrium and ventricle of your heart. That all just collapse at once, when the moment's right.

You don't need to see everything to know. You know because you know.

GUT

MISSED

Maybe it's this. Maybe it's not. It doesn't have to be perfect. We can fill in the gaps, to take a step. RD was her only child, left to her by her wife. Both breasts came off together, terrifyingly fast. Then came the chemo. RD sat next to his mother with ice chips and candies infused with palliative oils. RD watched his mother die, regardless.

She ignored it at first. His remaining mother. The things that went missing. The remaining tramadol. The cash. His mother's laptop. Who could blame him for wanting relief? She wanted relief. She paid him extra, so he'd stop. Taking things. So he wouldn't get into trouble elsewhere. The cops had brought him back once already, for stealing batteries and a bottle of Coke. He wasn't a kid, at nineteen, but it was a small town. When her truck went missing, she started to call them, then stopped. The truck came back in a week, and so did he.

It was the twin engines that did it. The twin engines did not come back. You're not setting foot on my boat until you're clean. She changed the locks on her house. When he broke in, she gave him money for rehab. She crawled out of a closet covered in her own vomit to do this, to hand it to him, cash she had hidden in a shoe. She was done, she said. She wouldn't do this anymore. Go get help.

It took him two weeks to die, after that. On another boat.

This boy she and her wife had fought so hard for. This boy they had cradled like the rarest of things.

Which of us is worse?

REASSEMBLE

He'll need to wake up eventually.

The stick-on letters, spread before me, dance around in my head.

Maybe she thought she could redo things to the point of self-forgiveness. Receive him. Watch him. Keep him, at least, from dying. Maybe she lives in terror of what will happen to me and Agnes. If she lets him out of her sight.

She knew at a glance what she was being given. Once you've loved one, you know. You must know the wife of one, too, from a distance of leagues, across whatever chop, despite what they try to show you.

But she must. Let him out of her sight. However briefly. It comes from somewhere.

The white letters coalesce and separate. Line up, and scatter. The white letters fail. It might be different, without a child.

AUSGRABEN

Suspicions about a neighbor, the sounds of dogs at night being not what they seem. Something I suspect is code.

Delete.

You're a paranoid schizophrenic, Dad, and need help. But I am not. I know what ground is beneath my feet.

We don't have what we need for an apartment. I click, instead, on *Community.*

The stump gave over at the touch of my foot. Beneath it, two filthy plastic bags.

I thought it looked odd. And so close to where I hid the dead-man's key.

Inside one bag: two tens, a five, and a one. Inside the other: what you'd expect. If you're someone with eyes in your head.

You know the needle tree? Agnes said.

Needle tree?

The tree with needles under it.

That's all of them. You'll have to be more specific.

Mama!

I'm sorry! I don't know which one. Anyway, what about it?

That's where me and Papa go.

Wow, I think I said, sliding from sink to stove to turn down the heat. Sounds really cool. Something to that mindless effect.

I'm at the table, with the stickers, and his hands are on the back of my neck. You okay? He gives a little squeeze. I must be as hard as rock.

I'm not the way he left me.

CLEAVE

We're five dark humps on the dock. Me, Agnes, and the three giant trash bags full of what we've taken. While we wait, in the gentle dark of the morning. The dory would cause us problems.

There's $400 on the table. Enough to save him, maybe. Not enough to kill him, I hope.

What could I write, but what he already knows? That the baneberry isn't the problem.

Sharon doesn't bother to cut the engine as I hoist the bags, then Agnes, over her gunwale. She's calm—like the day was meant for this. Though I didn't tell her it was coming.

Long Plank? I know she'll know it.

She nods.

I found it on the wall. On the map. About ten more islands out to sea. A long, skinny thing, like you'd think.

The posting said it's on the ferry line. There's a small market, a bed-and-breakfast, a school with ten kids, and a notary public who answers his door until nine.

The woman needs help with her horses in exchange for room and board.

We curve around the point, to the back side of Shepherd, and head out toward the sound. I know just what we look like from there. From that rock. From that beach.

GET HELP. SOMEONE WILL LOVE YOU AGAIN.

Sharon takes us across.

KNEES

FORGE

It's absurd that anyone up here goes for a winter foal—a foal should be born into the warmth of spring. But January foals bring more money at sale. In this unwelcoming place, the owner stands to lose as much as she stands to gain.

Before she left to spend the winter months in Virginia Beach—an escape she blamed on worsening arthritis—she kept the mare under lights, fooling her body into early estrus. The foal came out easily. The foal may freeze to death. Agnes and I are here, adding our heat to the mix. How much does she need the extra money? It's hard to tell with people. What they have, what they go without. What I wonder, mostly, as I finger her coats, slide open drawers to see what they hold, is if she can pay me.

I had a feeling, from the way this mare pawed her abdomen as parturition came on, that she wasn't going to take to the foal. I may have had a feeling before that. From meeting her.

Agnes is calm as she rests her body along the scrawny chestnut, who's back down for a nap. I'll go to them shortly. For now, I'm stroking the mare's long, hot neck. I've checked her for mastitis. I've got her baby's scent on my hands, am hoping to see her nostrils flare as she picks up something familiar. They don't. But she accepts my strokes. It's not that she didn't see what was on the ground, when they were together. She just didn't make anything of it, until I stroked his glistening head with a wet rag, imitating her tongue, to get him to stand. That's when she reared.

She lets me milk her. I bring the bottles to Agnes and let her feed the foal; consolation for not being allowed in here. Either of them.

The scene's not really mine either, I assure her, now.

We can't see the ferry from here, from this far side of the island. But we can hear it blast its horn as it shoves off from the pier, twice a day.

BEND

It's what they say, in the basement where I go to hear it, every Wednesday at 11:00 a.m. An hour-long ferry ride in each direction.

Even if you should have? I asked, the first time. No one gives credence to my doubts. You don't know what you don't know, they repeat and attest. Until you're ready to know it.

Until *who* says you're ready to know it?

You're alive, aren't you? They say. You're here.

Agnes is dishing up a slice of plastic pizza topped with plastic mushrooms in the plastic kitchen in the corner.

They tell me, again, the horrible things they put their own children through. Or parents. Themselves. They *laugh*, telling it.

You'll get here, they say.

You still don't know, someone added. But you know enough.

What the posting didn't advertise is that in the school building there's a computer attached to the internet, available to the public between the hours of 6:00 and 8:00 p.m.

HEW

She has a house on a lake. My mother. When the calls of the loons shorten from the hysteric elongations of night into short, puppylike yips, she knows it's almost morning. If she hears a whip-poor-will at midday, she knows there's something wrong with the bird. She works four days a week as a dental assistant, and four dogs wait for her at home. She might get another. She enjoys sugar in her coffee, and wine in the evening. Her favorite show is *Murphy Brown*, which she can watch because of the internet—she doesn't mind being late to the party, is just happy to be there. She brought two humans into the world, and that, too, is good.

It's too early to see Paul just yet.

People must see us, bundled up against the cold. Agnes steering from my lap, our hoods cinched tight around our faces, driving our small forklift down the narrow road as we go to collect the feed that's loaded off the ferry in fifty-pound bags. They must wonder, again, what we are. Must try to see us through the frost clinging to their lashes. We have it, too; the wool shrouds around our faces sending our liquid breath upward to freeze.

•

This foal won't race. He'll always be weak. He certainly won't get the owner whatever extra she needed. I tell her gently, on the phone. Wondering if she'll fly back. If we'll lose our place.

We'll see, is what she says. Feed him well. Please do whatever you can.

Breathe, Mama.

I stroke the mare again and let her know it's all okay. I squeeze between her ears, working at the rock of muscle.

She didn't ask for this.

I put my body under the blanket.

His body, I think, is getting warmer. His body is more relaxed. Agnes is asleep, so I remind myself to breathe.

She's up in the loft, where the heat of the horses collects. She's under a pile of blankets, a hot water bottle inside the curve of her. She refuses to sleep in the house, without me. She's fine, I think.

We'll live here for the week, until he can make it through the night alone. We'll give him the best chance we can, then we'll find a way to make this other person's home our own.

On Reddit:

> *Any other k users out there piss hot for hydrocodone??*
>   *Where u buy from bro it can be cut, don't u think they want u coming back?*

Ya, I used k for a year no problem then did a screen for a job and came up for methadone and was like what? Im not suprised tho.

> *I tried a new "enhanced" product and immediately knew something wasn't right, it was my girlfriend who suggested I pick up a 12-panel from Walgreens. It showed fentanyl and I vowed to not order from that company again. My girlfriend thought I was an idiot and I literally had to take her to the website and show her I wasn't missing anything, that I didn't miss any "code words" like she thought there would be. It's all good now, but I'm glad I didn't like the way I felt.*

I remember the back rooms.

How did it go: kratom, kratom cut with hydrocodone or methadone or fentanyl, then heroin? Or heroin, kratom cut with whatever, then heroin again? Or something else? When did he know what he was taking?

You'll never know! the basement people say. But you know enough. You know what you had to do.

I made a vow, I say.

No one knows what a marriage will call for. The woman who says this never speaks, and is the type of woman who might sit all day in the reading room of the library, unnoticed.

I don't, though, I think. Know enough. Because in one version, it's my fault. In one version, I drove him to heroin, to the street, to wherever he is now. To what he could procure quickly, with cash.

I've never been to a lobster pound. I don't know how high or wide the bodies are stacked. How loud or muted the sound of their collective scuttling, of their useless claws dragging over shell.

We're shoveling a path to the pasture. Through deep, crusted snow. And we hear a great slapping—once, then twice—out on the open water, beyond sight.

Her eyes go wide, and she looks at me: Whales are born in winter, too?

Pilot whales only, I say.

Out there, in the frigid quiet of the open pasture, is all of it: the brittle grass, the frozen manure, the low-moving night animals, the sound of ocean slapping cliff, the tolling of a ledge bell, the low rumble of a passing oil tanker; all of it heard, no doubt, by the other islanders, tucked in, guns and savings beneath their beds. Out there, my focus can dissolve and crystallize; I can become a part of it—a mind like stars, everywhere.

Here, underneath this blanket, inside the walls of this

stable, it's me and the pounding of this boy's heart, which is everything, until I notice my own.

What the hammer? what the chain,
In what furnace was thy brain?

Seeing is not the same as making. I can't make her; can only show her how it's done.

Oh, Agnes. I must steal a bit of myself back.

ACKNOWLEDGMENTS

I'd like to thank this book's earliest supporters—namely, my partner in life, and the kindest man I've ever known, Adam Stockman (who had every practical reason to dissuade me from biting it off), and the clear-eyed Sarah Bowlin, whose endlessly perfect questions helped it find footing. And everyone who read a draft at some point along the line—Julia (J.J.) Gersen and Lewis Robinson and Liz Solms and Stacey Solie, all of whom said to keep going, or something I interpreted that way. Thanks to Griffin Leschefske at Pierce Atwood who helped me—a stranger—understand the potentialities of probate. To Susan Reed, who I only ever hoped would help my nerve pain, but who taught me to see trees for their backbones. And to everyone, especially, who cared for my little bug while I focused my attention here. You know who you are, and I love you. Thank you to my employers for being flexible. Thank you to the Portland Public Library for providing what the internet can't.

Finally, my deepest gratitude to Kendall Storey, my fearless editor, who saw potential in the mess of the original pages, and trusted me to make right of them, offering clearheaded guidance along the way that sometimes sank in a little late—because that is how I operate.

Thank you, my child, for tolerating the theft, as best you were able.

MEGHAN GILLISS attended the Bennington Writing Seminars and is a fellow of the Hewnoaks Artist Colony. Her short fiction has appeared in *Salamander, Nat. Brut, The Rattling Wall, fields, North by Northeast: New Short Fiction by Writers from Maine and New England*, and *New Letters*, which awarded her the Alexander Patterson Cappon Prize for Fiction. She has worked as a journalist, a bookseller, a librarian, and a hospital worker, and lives in Portland, Maine. *Lungfish* is her first novel.